THE FORGOTTEN VOICES OF JANE DARK

THE FORGOTTEN VOICES OF JANE DARK

Sarah Murphy

PEDLAR
PRESS

PEDLAR PRESS
PO Box 26, Station P, Toronto Ontario M5S 2S6 Canada

ACKNOWLEDGEMENTS. The publisher gratefully acknowledges the financial support of the Canada Council for the Arts and the Ontario Arts Council for its publishing program.

The author wishes to acknowledge the support of the Canada Council for the Arts and the Alberta Foundation for the Arts.

The following stories have appeared previously, often in slightly different versions, in the following publications: "Survivor" has appeared in *Paragraph*; "This Blanket of Dismemberment" in *Tessera*; "Balancing Act" in *Grain* and *Alberta Unbound*; "Once Upon a Time" in *Eating Apples*.

NATIONAL LIBRARY OF CANADA CATALOGUING IN PUBLICATION

Murphy, Sarah, 1946-
    The forgotten voices of Jane Dark / Sarah Murphy. -- 1st ed.

ISBN 0-9732140-4-X

1. Child sexual abuse--Fiction. 2. Murphy, Sarah, 1946-. 3. Adult child sexual abuse victims--Biography. 4. Authors, Canadian (English)--20th century--Biography. I. Title.

PS8576.U67F67 2003   C813'.54   C2003-905105-6

First Edition

DESIGN Zab Design & Typography
COVER ART Margaux Williamson
Printed in Canada

For Tom Proudlock

1944 – 2000

You made my millennium

MEMORY

It will be a simple conversation. This one in the East Kootenays. A restaurant. A family meal. A day like any other. A child's drawing day. The sky, sky blue. The grass, grass green. Stereotypical, the clouds meander across the movie screen of your eyes, the mountains arising as if behind.

And it will be only at the very beginning of this, when your eyes, your hands, your mind have only just begun to rebel and to refuse you comfort. Your days to appear as through a grey screen.

You will speak only to make time pass. You all will. As you wait on the open balcony for lunch to be served and to be eaten and to be over and to be on your way back to Calgary. Already, in mid-fall, no matter the blue of the sky around you, today you must calculate for snow in the high mountain passes.

They may come from this, those remarks on the mathematical imagination. That somehow in the way you move your salad around with your fork you are attempting to create a pattern. Perhaps to predict the snow. Or whether or not you will encounter a caterpillar, or some foreign object. It's a joke for you. As for your friends. Your foreign object, your strange creature incidence rate so far above the norm. They try to find in it a corollary for Murphy's law. Joke how they like to eat with you because between ladybugs and rubber spatulas maybe they'll score a free bottle of wine. The way it will go that day with the staple. Only this time it is just the conversation that is sharp edged, or full of small soft-bodied things.

Redolent with hidden threats you will not understand until much later.

Maybe it is the memory of your friend Jean which brings it up. Which takes it from mathematics to memory — to mathematics and memory. She was your closest friend in high school, the other outcast, the one with whom you refused to live the story of The Makeover. The one with whom you lived on the edge, somewhere between beat and hip as the sixties began and you to work in its movements. Jean, the brilliant poet and actress who loved not the precision but the concrete individuality of numbers, the magic of their pull, their attraction, as if already she assigned them charm or spin or strangeness like quarks. A Maya sensibility if you ever met one, that singing the praises of number. Only she cracked up her third year doing off Broadway, cracked, and never recovered.

You think about it a lot off and on, the secret life of numbers, the numbered life of secrets. For Jean who loved word play too, and taught you difference and frame of reference and postmodernity on the swings in Central Park at the age of fifteen — the hidden systems inside things. Until you once joined her inside her secret system, trying to forget how the hiding and unhiding of things might pertain to yourself.

You do not speak of this but quite objectively of the function of system in schizophrenia and personality disorders, then go on to mention the Russian — much studied, perhaps apocryphal — who remembered everything. Not the gift of total recall you say, laughing, since it is obvious he recalled nothing. Nothing ever went far enough away to need to be called back, but was present all the time. Without relief. So the curse of eternal presence then. With everything that had ever happened, or been reported, with him at all times, until he was rendered unable to function by the cacophony of his mind, by all those details clamouring for attention. Destroyed by his inability to order, to priorize and thereby to repress, to suppress, at least locally, at least for a time, memory. Like you might place things in a file drawer, or under a computer directory, giving them an address you can write to. While you momentarily work on something else.

The way you try to calculate the possibility of snow from the whiteness of the mountains. If there is even the faintest line of clouds along their tops.

Momentarily, you will forget the conversation.

Your mother sits opposite you. Tom to your left. Your younger son in a booster chair to your right. Your daughter is somewhere outside smoking. It will be your mother who speaks. Turning herself away toward the mountains, her hair glinting as white as the early snow on the peaks, so that you will see her in profile, like that one photograph of her your brother will send years later. It is the last time you will invite her to visit — though you do not know that yet — as she says, how awful having such a memory would be. And she does not speak of the failure to priorize. Or of sorting events for future recall.

Dreadful. Dreadful. She will say, shaking her head: Dreadful. The most important task in life is to forget. Only forgetting allows us to survive.

Later, moving her fork through her food, echoing yours, her voice still determined, authoritative, she will go on. I am convinced, she will say, as you will stare at her, the hunched back, the thinning hair, the wrinkled age-spotted hands, the body collapsing in on itself in advancing osteoporosis. I am convinced, she will repeat, someone not at all the woman who haunts your dreams, who soon will haunt your waking moments, brown to grey haired, lipstick bright or smeared, erect or rubber body drunk. Though you will feel the energy of that haunting in her words. I am convinced, repeated yet again. I am convinced that we die from the weight of our memories.

Then stating simply, spreading her hands, their multitude of silver rings glinting: We remember too much.

Too much.

You will notice the weight of time on her. And feel the slow spreading purple sickness in your belly. Knowing but not knowing what it is. The way, you will think later, you always have. Feel it in the way you put yourself on hold whenever she's around. The way you have since you started leaving home at fourteen. Or maybe that's just the first time you were able to notice it, because those times were the first times wherein you didn't have to do it, hold all the muscles of your body tense, your mind waiting, for the explosion to come. Only maybe that's not true either.

Maybe it goes much further back. Dictates the difference in how you imagine the fences you balanced on, the grass below them so very green, the school you went to, the colours of the books in its library so very bright, and your room, your house, so grey on grey.

You think briefly then of all the time you spent in fear of her. Of the moment she could change and become other. Change and attack. You, no longer the bright, beloved daughter who just had to be brought into line, but the stupid cunt who ought to just shut up and die. All the things you have always known but put away, saying she doesn't really mean it, or I'm strong I can take it, her misery and her pain. Willing to cover it all up because you needed that part-time good mother. The one sitting opposite you.

You notice what you will not say. That if we died of what we remember then she would be Dorian Gray. Looking forever young. Only you would be the portrait in the closet, hidden where you always were, there or in your brother's room, where there was a lock, when it got too late before she came home. No, it is not memory this weight of age, though maybe its traces, the poisonous residue of her unacknowledged, her forgotten, actions. Imploding the vessel of her body.

You will think of Acquired Immune Deficiency Syndrome, and the failure of the memory clones of the t-cells to reproduce their knowledge of the virus. Of any virus. Of anything. Body memory disappearing at its most basic. Truly, you think, it is memory loss that kills. If we do not remember we dissolve ourselves, fail to know the difference between self and surround, self and other. Fail to retain the information with which, day after day, we delimit ourselves, to make ourselves anew.

If we do not remember we are already dead, you will hear yourself whisper under your breath, not daring to speak aloud.

All of it will be a jumble. Her. Not her. Her words. Not her words. You. Not you. To be gone over then, to be gone over later, to be remembered, to be forgotten. To be remembered and forgotten again. The way memory is ordered. To order the self.

There sometimes. Gone sometimes. Weighing down our cells. Tiring them. Just as she says. Grinding them into chaos.

You will feel it. The way you did even as you balanced on the steel half-circle of your favourite fence: the pain against the properly blue sky, the stereotypical green grass, the white glimmer of the mountains. And inside your mind in the brightness of those bursts of light that leave their grey aftershadow. The pain of memory unremembered. Until looking at her, you wonder if it is something you, too, could die of.

Only you know it will not be memory, not as we know it when we say, I remember, but memory unrecalled, what cannot be called into mind, but instead waits for us, as you wait for it. The torpedo that always detonates at the sudden sight, the smell, the sound, of forgotten things. And pulls them forward. And rushes them away. Like the voices in your mind, the ones that have been there as long as you have memory, but that are louder now, causing you to shake your head back and forth: guardians of a different order, a different need. Speaking, babbling, in tones almost there, almost erased. Barely at the edge of recall. The voices of Jane Dark. Voices for a grey room.

The purple will detonate. Going off in you. Deep inside. Exploding to your edges: red, yellow, blue like a cartoon. Forcing an orange then a grey curtain before your eyes. Leaving you there. With the grey. The familiar grey world that took up your entire adolescence. You have remembered that for years. That grey. How even on the National Executive Committee of the Students for a Democratic Society, your friends said you never smiled. What probably gained you your position on the National Executive Committee, at sixteen, you, the only female. You were just so damned serious. So damned earnest. Only years later would another woman, excluded, tell you she thought that serious way you did all tasks, took on all comers, was Catholic guilt. No, you said. You had been building a future, recruiting help for when the explosions came, creating a place to go, people who would protect you. With your mind. The way other women did with their bodies.

Yet the grey did drive you to become an artist. To move to Mexico, win art prizes, learn Spanish. Where at last it gave way. Under the weight of your work with colours. And of your freedom. You, finally, your own protection. Free of waiting. The grey world of waiting. Of waiting to be free of waiting. Only now you are waiting again. This time for the voices. The memories.

It is only later, safe home over the passes without incident, ready to go to sleep in your own bed, yet with that same vigilance in your body, even with Tom next to you, that you will think how familiar it is. How each night you were home you waited for the attack to come. How with your mother downstairs, you wait again. To wake up startled. The way you did to the poker about to descend on your head, wielded by her hand. Only now it is your mind, your memories of her. A thought, or an image, always ready to descend on your head. You wake up suffocated. Terrified of her body. And of being pushed into that place. By one more image you can't yet recognize. But that will come back again.

After she leaves. This one, last time.

In the restaurant you will take a deep breath. This time too, you have made your decision. You will let it go. And it is not only fear, but the twisting pity you have always felt, that makes you do it. Unwilling to spoil the day, the passes yet to come, whether fresh snow or pine needles against mossy ground, with ugly, indecipherable, complex emotions. The way you always feel dirty yourself, having attacked. Even if you know, this time at least, it would barely have been an attack at all. As you become, yourself, momentarily, one of those whispered voices.

Except that at least you will be sure that this whisper is true.

Soon the memory of this afternoon will be forgotten, too.

Thought inconsequential and filed away under things you have always known but prefer not to bother with. Only to be picked up again years later, when most of the work you must do with memory in order to survive has been done, when you will find that remark written down in your journal.

After you have remembered, and forgotten again and remembered and forgotten and remembered, the bursts of pain coming more regularly, more urgently, more horribly, like years of prolonged labour, until at last you will start to write them down so they will always be there, present in the world, independent of your memory: All those things done to you in the nights of her drinking. The ones you had always known, and the ones you had committed to a depth of forgetting. To leave only the traces of their harm in your mind and body.

Above all you will remember how, day after day, in the tumult of your childhood, she, your Scheherazade, told her 1001 stories not the night before but the morning after. Using them to commit not just herself, but those around her, you, your brother, her friends, to forgetting with her. Saying time after time when you would bring up what had happened, or ask why it had happened, that she could not remember. After which she would tell a story of her own suffering. Perhaps adding how much she loved you.

You will find these things written, too. Like the letter you wrote on your sixteenth birthday. When you returned home after days of being away, of staying with friends, and — a birthday present to yourself you think now — you tried to give it to her. A letter that detailed the men coming to your room at night, men who, again, you had forgotten. Until one day, you did it again, when, as angry as you had been when you wrote the letter, you detailed enough of the incidents for your therapist to note how interesting it was that you knew so much more when you were angry. Though he did not go so far as to suggest you try for that state very often.

While you will find that letter too, hidden in the oldest of your adolescent journals, like so much, even that afternoon's remark, you had hidden away.

Though, if asked of the day you turned sixteen, you would remember how your mother gave you a tiny — and lovely — silver pendant, of the kind you could buy for a dollar then in the Village — you can still smell those shops — and how she had told you that she loved you. And you can still see yourself, at the bottom of the stair, while she was at the top, telling you how she didn't want to listen to you, couldn't listen to you, her life had been so difficult, she loved you too much to listen to you.

She had been so desperate, how could she do anything else but forget.

Even knowing that you were being manipulated, you accepted the explanation through your tears, put the letter back in your purse and turned away. And thought yourself strong enough to do the remembering for both of you, to bear that killer burden. Even if you, too, would then forget. Thinking, just as she will tell you those years later, that forgetting was the only way to save not just her, but your world, your life.

The ideas of those years would both help and hinder. It was important to come to know, even in the silence of your pity, that she is, after all, just one image. And not of power and strength, but of horror and defeat. Of a woman twisted, like so many others, male and female, denied her realization, into striking out to destroy what lies within her reach. In her case, her children. The origin of that one image: childeater.

It is feminism's close examination of that idea which will free you from the belief that her fate would have to be yours if you tried to go beyond woman's narrowly defined fifties role. The way you started to do early on in the SDS, but still convinced you had to be a perfect bitch: Or a man. Later you would understand that even ideologically you did not have to stake your fate on hers. Though it will take a much longer time to get beyond the facile version of feminism which would make you believe that you had always to carry your mother with you. Thinking to heal her. Or that there was something wrong with you if you could not do it: Heal the mother daughter bond. To make the tension in your body doubly your fault, for being there and for leaving you unable to embrace her.

She would say it too, sometimes, laughing at you. Drunk or sober, tell you she was your challenge. And that if you were woman enough, you would do it. Carry her with you. You remember all the things she wished you to do for her. Your academic achievements. Your early public persona. Though you were always too radical. Too over the top. Took too many risks. Making her throw your drawings out into the street. Make drunken fun of your convictions, your language. Assault your friends.

The story that contained only pendants and occasional Aunty Mame style drinking bouts was the only way to tell your world so that not only she, but you, would not be shameful, bad. The only way that would let you form yourself as a coherent, a good, an intelligent person, and get away. After all, you could be none of those and still be part of this. So that it was the only way not to be detonated, dismembered, into the incoherent dissolving pain of her nights. And what she did to you in them, that had dissolved you, too. Some part of you.

The years you agreed with her, that even presence, presence in your body, much less memory, would kill you. Kill you all. That the only way to save the good mother, the one you needed to believe in in order to believe in yourself, the one who visited her body sometimes by day, the one you wished to keep, was to join her in this quest. To be her squire, her yeoman, on the journey to forgetting.

You will see too, how even when you remembered you forgot. Shrugging your shoulders over and over for years. Still telling yourself you were strong. And this. This shame. It did not matter. It had not affected you. And if the child in you was dead, or came out only to draw through your hands. Still. You had gotten more than most. There were good years. You were here. After all. More or less. And you had to be grateful for that.

Even if there were always memories that would make you shiver as with a fever. Seeing the danger in the shadow. The other occult meaning of naming the monster, not to control it, but to give it its opportunity to control you. That with naming you call it into your presence, in all its power. And you fearing, against all reason, that if you said even to yourself, clearly who she was, you would be devoured, then become her. So that maybe it was still best to think about it tomorrow. And forget Tara, just never go back home at all. Not even in your mind.

Until, all this will surface, and for a period of more than two years you will live in such darkness, such pain, that you think it has already happened: you have died from the weight of your memories. This is when you will look through your journal, and see her words, there on the page, and remember forgetting instead of forget remembering. When you will finally acknowledge that remembering, remembering as much as you can, will become the only way to save yourself. To declare who you are.

Finally, you will recognize that you are neither her, nor what she has done to you.

SURVIVOR

This is where you will start, or so it might seem, the first time you remember. It will be your own room. You, now. An adult. The child will be your child. The man, your husband. But it will be hard to know that.

❧ ❧ ❧

Imagine it, then. Somewhere. Anywhere. Lost in space. Or time. In the time of your life.

A bed. A man. A child. The man's hand over the child's mouth. Yet the child is not screaming. In fact, there is no attempt to scream. This is a game. The parent's hand over the child's mouth. A game. That the child is playing.

I want, the child says. Then pushes the mouth into the hand to stop the word of wanting from coming out.

The child is laughing. It is fun this game of stopping the word, of stopping the desire, from coming out. Fun. With the laugh rising to a scream. Inside the shelter of the hand. A scream of delight without words. So much fun. This silence rewarded.

By the touch of the hand.

❀ ❀ ❀

Silence growing, enormous as she watches. The two of them. Man and child. The three of us, she could say. Man woman and child. With the woman watching.

She is the only one who is afraid. The only one who places her hand on her throat. The only one who says, Stop. Without knowing why she says: Stop. Just, Stop, stop. A word against the silence. Her word against the silence. The word against her silence. The silence growing.

Stop. Stop. She shakes her head. They do not understand.

It was a game, the man says. A game.

She knows this. It was clear there was no restraint. And the joy in the child. She could see it. Just the child, freely, moving his head into the hand. Freely. Freely.

The child, crying now, I want, I want, still without a word, the word forgotten in his need for the hand to stop the word. And this thing the child does not yet know how to say: I did not wish the game to stop, I did not. As she leans against the wall shaking, as they both look at her. The man and the child.

What is this? Why has she ended the game?

❀ ❀ ❀

The beginning of the answer is to know that the story is unknown. The beginning of the answer is to know that you do not necessarily wish to know the story. The beginning of the answer is to know that no one knows if there is a story.

That when you say, Stop! you raise up your hand, a hand for the child to run into.

You will remember that hand. How you have raised it. Again and again. Perhaps there is a child you will remember as well. Not your child, the child on the bed, but a child that is you. Still lost somewhere. Among so many hands. Raised or pushing. Grabbing too. Or rubbing. Held out. Waiting.

You will imagine it again. Try to hold on.

✿ ✿ ✿

Her head still against the wall, she covers her mouth with her hand. Looks down. Looks away.

I just don't know, she says. I don't know. It just scared me, that's all. It just scared me. I know that nothing was wrong. I know that it was a game. But it scared me. It scared me.

Don't talk into your hand, he says. How can I understand you if you put your hand over your mouth.

✿ ✿ ✿

They will leave then. The man and the child. On to lunch. And to other games. In the backyard. She will smile as they go. And remove her hand a moment from her mouth. To wave. Listening to their promise to call her when lunch is ready.

Then she will put her hand back over her mouth. So they do not hear her crying. Or ask further questions.

✿ ✿ ✿

It is hard to say what it is, then. This thing she feels. That you feel for her. If it is not a story. After all, the elements are present. At least some. A plot. A mystery. To be found and solved.

At least resolved. Spoken about, let go.

But it is hard to let go. Harder even, to speak. Especially if you do not know the secret. How can you let go of a secret you don't know. Plot a mystery whose ending is unclear. Tell a story whose resolution is shrouded. Learn a lesson from it because you know the lesson is there. Whenever you want it. Like a book you can reopen. How can you open a book whose title you don't even know?

❀ ❀ ❀

She looks at the book next to her pillow. She can open that, if she wants. A simple act: Because it is there. Hunting the Quark, the book is called. Perhaps this is like that. Perhaps it is all particle traces in a cloud chamber. Perhaps that is one way to look at it.

Forget the secret, remember the effects of the moment of collision. Or just that there was one.

With particles sent out as close to the speed of light as possible from the mouth of the cyclotron. The cyclotron, like life itself, a spiral. With a particle, gaining momentum as it circles. As it is shot out from a lonely to a crowded space in order to collide.

❀ ❀ ❀

What makes it still harder to know what happens now is that it is not clear which particle you would be. The one that moves faster and faster, a child into a hand, or just the one that waits. As the hand closes with the child, inexorably.

What is clear is that there was a collision. And a shattering. Into fragments. Shattering.

And a trace, perhaps only a small trace, but a trace. Traces. Of the child she has felt, the child you have felt, her hand over her mouth.

Find her, a voice in your mind says.
Solve for her.

❀ ❀ ❀

You felt her today. Not the woman you imagine being you, the way you always have, imagining her, forming her, formulating her. Trying to watch yourself from outside your body. But the child who is you. Unmarked. Or unremarked. Perhaps you without your name. A particle. Part of you, without even part of your name. The hidden child you never thought you would wish to remember. Like a file whose name has been deleted from the directory. You know this problem well from your computer: Impossible to recall.

But still there. A shift in the electronic pattern. A child who draws pictures in her mind. In your mind. A child who remembers a hand. Who draws it for you. Bright against your closed eyes.

❀ ❀ ❀

Trajectory, the book asserts, is determined by energy present in the collision. And the number of particles in the disintegration. From that a lot can be calculated. As long as there is charge. As long as the particle, the one you want, has charge, its movement will ionize particles in the chamber. To create a visible trajectory. If it does not have charge, you must surmise the particle's nature. Everything about it. Even its number. Whether it is truly one, or more than one. Whether you are one, or more than one. He or she, it or they. From the particles that do have charge, whose trajectory is known.

❀ ❀ ❀

She believes that she has charge. That woman you imagine, her hand over her mouth, that is you sitting on the bed. With or without a name, the one you have always mistaken for yourself. Moving back and forth. Still tempted toward sobbing.

She believes she has affected things. Not simply been affected by them. Her trajectory can be seen, her mass calculated by the distance she has travelled. She is sure of that. At least that: She thinks she is clearly visible.

She does not know about other qualities, or other particles that may have scattered with her, who or what they are, if they are her or not her. You or not you. The child or not the child. Or if they could be so easily seen. If it is just a matter of looking closely. Or of making careful calculations. It is like the story that is not a story, this collision which is a secret which has created her trajectory.

The one you carry forward into the years.

❖ ❖ ❖

The lack of texture, of specificity, will rankle. It will be hard to feel this thing. In order to know where to begin. To find the elements in the equation. To try to draw it or describe it. Find other ways to make it real.

To move back along the trajectory. Among the clouds, the ions, it will be hard to know you move at all. Toward that moment. Or moments. To find the time, place, look, smell, sound. Something more than this sensation like reading braille. Your life like raised lumps on a white sheet, barely casting shadows. And your fingers too numb to discern their exact location: Their meaning.

You will want more than description. Names, dates. External evidence. To find the others. The particles you cannot name. Even as you. Or not you.

The collision of a child, with. . . a hand, a mouth? With what with who, with how many? With ... ?

With the fear that she feels even as she reaches across the bed. Not just as she watches the child's face, the man's hand. But as she touches the child's chest.

Later. When she joins them in the yard. Trying to smile again. To make it all right. When she picks the child up. Kisses him on the head. Everything all right now. Only she feels the shiver. The recoil. Not in him. In her. Moving up her arms where they touch his chest, his nipples. To inhabit her own. To squeeze. At the place she now has breasts. Even as the child smiles. And she puts him down. Ignoring the pain in her chest.

❖ ❖ ❖

From that shiver moving up the hand could perhaps be surmised more about the collision. If she has Charm, or Flavour, or Colour.

Strangeness perhaps. Definitely negative spin. Clearly. Something even the child can feel. As he comes to rest again. Feet on the ground.

Looking at the artificial smoothness of her face. As she attempts not to scream.

❖ ❖ ❖

Perhaps you can create the rest. After all, science is like that too. That is what her book will tell you. The eight-fold way of those particles imagined that cannot be seen. How they are mathematically extrapolated. Through their harmony. Like the music of the spheres. Beauty in quarks that barely give evidence of their presence.

Perhaps that is the way to find the others. Those present in the collision. Present after the collision. Create their texture. Locate yourself.

❖ ❖ ❖

Make the elements harmonious. Beautiful in order to see them. Well-shaped, well-constructed. Moulded like a tin ceiling. Polished like floor tiles. Warm like a gas fire.

Work image by brilliant image.

Attach the hand to a wrist to an arm to a shoulder to a head with a face. Feel the intent: To play, to suffocate, to silence, to terrify, to love, to caress, to hurt, to punish, to comfort, to force, to abuse.

❖ ❖ ❖

Only somewhere in there, soon, or not so very soon, you know this already, the harmony will break down. The system will not bear the weight of so many elements in contradiction. With the feelings attached to them like the ionized particles among the water vapour.

But too many. Ionizing the whole field. Clouding the whole chamber. So that nothing is visible. Nothing at all.

Life is not like science. Not in this. Science does not hurt. Not of itself.

❖ ❖ ❖

The man is still waiting. Standing by the barbecue. Spatula in hand. Not for the food to cook. But for an answer. Even if the child has forgotten the game. Or how she stopped it. With her voice.

The man looks over at her. He still wants to know what happened. She shakes her head again. He has noticed where her tears still mark her face.

❖ ❖ ❖

She does remember a tin ceiling. And a window. White floor tiles. Mixed with brown. Other colours. Blue and green and grey. Like a cloud chamber or a night terror. The feeling of suffocation. And people laughing. Laughing at her. At the child who will not be remembered. Asking her to do something she does not wish to do. Doing to her something she does not wish done. The faces looking down at her. Laughing.

And a penis enlarged to the size of a movie screen.

❖ ❖ ❖

There is little more. Except fear. The fear is always there. It has texture. Fierce and enduring. The only thing whose possession of Charm or Flavour or Colour might be determined. Whose trajectory continues. Apart from her. From you. Droning on. A hum like cicadas. Or high tension wires.

Now. In the bedroom. Or the yard. In the kitchen. Among the plants.

And the hand raised. That continues too. Always. The one that says, Stop! And the mouth that pushes into it. Hiding its word.

❖ ❖ ❖

It is comforting that hand. Warm. Sheltering. It accompanies her. It is hard to remove from her mouth.

To let her speak.

❖ ❖ ❖

A year from now you will look back. It will not be the first time you remember. You will have remembered often. And now too, you will remember that you have remembered.

But you will be in the same place. In the bedroom.

Where still, you will think of quarks and cloud chambers. And trajectories. Though it's long ago you will have finished the book.

❖ ❖ ❖

And gone on to chaos theory. Systems in breakdown that bifurcate and bifurcate. Each one as valid as the next. And hands too, and rooms. Splitting and splitting. In many colours now. Some still blue and grey, some orange and yellow. One in strident shimmering acid green.

Until the days of blood come, red in the space that surrounds your eyes. A toy train that is stopped by the thunk of a head, the skull melon-like, hitting the floor. And somewhere a pool of blood. Crimson to indigo. Drying. The floor tiles beneath it a lighter red and blue. And the smell of tar. Of glue. Of urine.

And always the hands. And the laughter. Bright and dark. Dark and bright. Again and again. And the day for you most terrible of all: When the genitals as large as movie screens, as large as all the room in a child's vision, are not only those of men.

❖ ❖ ❖

When there will be a woman there, the genitalia perfectly drawn, not a movie, but a hyperrealist painting. What a camera could never do. Only the eye. And the mind behind it. Storing detail to avoid meaning. Or movement. Identification.

And the image no longer blue grey and dull. But orange and yellow. Too bright. Too bright.

Blinding.

❖ ❖ ❖

Some days you will still see yourself as the strange attractor. Introducing chaos into order. Thinking. That order was there always before you. That you yourself are the collision. The dissolution. The shattering. That it is your nature. Your only quality. Beyond the charge that makes you visible when you no longer wish to be seen. And negative spin.

Falling down and down and down. Your foot too often seeming to step through the ground, the sidewalk, the carpet, the linoleum. Into this place, these places, you will no longer wish to explore.

❖ ❖ ❖

Other days, you will know it is not your fault. Think: Whatever chaos there is in your universe, was not brought by you. Something did hit you. You did hit something. You will be sure of that. But then you will think: What was it? Who? Which one, where? And the apartment will come back, and the house, the ceiling tiles, and the fan. Brown grey, moving too fast to see.

And you will be exploring. Again. Purposeful. Following the hand. Always the hand. Bifurcating and bifurcating. Each system as valid as the other. But held to your mouth. Your mouth.

The you that was a child.

That was many children.

❖ ❖ ❖

Until you will know somehow. After a while. What will seem a very long while. With the memories coming back and back and back. Not so much haunting as possessing you. Uncountable bifurcated and distinct trajectories, splintered scenes, fragmented images. That beat at you, twist you, make you itch or burn, gag or throw up. Over and over.

That still: You will not dissolve.
You are too solid for this chaos. Too durable.

❋ ❋ ❋

Something that you can call you has endured. Some you is still here. And will remain. You have your significance in the system. Whichever one it is. Positions as well as trajectories. Visible or invisible. One or many. From which to affect things. Even if you do not always know where you are.

You will smile then. And breathe more.

While the child, your child, older now, will smile too. And speak words easily.

❋ ❋ ❋

The same will not be true of her. The battering will have its effect. Her hand still over her mouth, she will fall too easily into silence. Often in mid-sentence. Mid-thought. Until you will hardly be able to imagine her speaking at all.

❋ ❋ ❋

But you will know more. Along with your durability will come this one small thing. You will know that now. Now. In this now when you are you. This now when you may allow yourself to be you. To call yourself by your name. That the hand is your own. And the mouth it covers.

What you do with them is your choice. Yours alone.

In that itself is power.

❋ ❋ ❋

Ooh wah, ooh wah, she will say. Sitting in that bedroom alone, abstracted, thinking. Ooh wah. Placing her hand over

her mouth, then removing it. Ooh, she hears as the hand
moves to the mouth. Wah, as it moves away.

❧ ❧ ❧

It is fun this game. The one the child has played. The hand
coming to the mouth, or the mouth to the hand. The mouth
sucking, the hand pulling away. Fun to hear the sounds come
out. Fun to pass the time.

Ooh wah, ooh wah, she repeats.

She remembers the child. Her child playing downstairs,
the voice shrill with laughter, penetrating to where she sits.
And too, the child that was her. Watchful eyes always watching. Wallpaper. Or ceiling tiles. A gas fire.

Tears spring to her eyes. Run down her cheeks.

Ooh wah, she repeats, ooh wah.

I want, she hears, I want.

Ooh wah. I want.

She laughs. And the room seems to expand. No longer
crushing her. She is, suddenly, momentarily, not afraid.

❧ ❧ ❧

Soon, too soon, the droning fear will resume. But you will
remember that moment. Give it a name. For future recall.

Some day when you know what comes next.

THIS BLANKET OF DISMEMBERMENT

I will answer your question, then. Yes, the girl I am watching sitting naked in the chair is me. The person sitting there is me. And she is very cold. Though the chair is big and grey and covered in thick cotton cloth and seems to surround her, her arms out on its arms, held unmoving, still: She is very cold. You can tell that from the gooseflesh along the arms and legs if you look closely. I will not look at the rest of her body, except maybe the protrusion of the rib cage on the left, a birth defect; instead I will cover it all with my thoughts, the way she tried to cover herself leaning forward over her knees, when they told her not to move, Don't move or we'll tie you up, her brother said, so that she smiled. Okay, she said. Pretend there is nothing to be afraid of and nothing will happen, I told her, uncurling her arms from where they wished to press against her legs and putting them back on the arms of the sofa. Don't worry, I said, so that she said it too. The one who was not her brother was masturbating on the couch. She pretended that did not interest her. That it was no more important than the television, or than being cold. If she noticed, maybe they would make her come over again and kiss it, maybe they would want more this time. I make her look at the ceiling.

That helps sometimes. If I make her concentrate on the things around her. The dirt under her fingernails, or the texture of the cotton under her fingers. Even under her bum. Though I don't like her to think about that part of her body, to notice it, or the cold rough cotton with its knots. If she thinks about that she might think about the part in front, exposed to the air now instead of rubbing against the smooth comforting texture of her underwear. And then she might squirm a little and they might think about it too, and ask her to open her legs again so they can look at it more closely. Open up, Sis, her brother might say, and then there's the possibility she might even feel something down there. She does when she plays with it herself, when she's alone. And that's the last thing I want. So, the wallpaper will do, this time. How the little ribbons curl around the flowers inside their cornucopias, that's a word they just taught me in school, it means horn of riches, like the flowers pouring out.

She seems very small over there. In the middle of that chair. Very very small. Like a doll. And so very skinny. There are no dolls like that. Not yet. Dolls are all fat baby dolls, or adolescent dolls with breasts but no nipples. She has nipples. But no breasts to speak of. I know that without looking. I won't look there. Not even for an instant. She would be better off if she were made like the dolls. Smooth plastic from neck to the joints of the thighs. Where her legs come forward. Squeezed together to cover that other part the dolls don't have. To try to pretend she doesn't have it either. The way I tell her to. Bend one hip into the chair, the other up toward the lamp, curve one shoulder in too, shrinking her.

Stop, don't move, they say.

It's obvious she has not shrunk enough since the last time, even if I have stopped feeding her. Except a little. I let her eat a bit. She keeps saying she wants more, but by now it seems to make her sick. Someone always wants to feed her something rich in iron, liver or spinach, even tomatoes. She's anemic they say. Anemic. Even her brother wants to feed her. Offering her things from his plate. But she just looks. At his plate heaped up with meat and vegetables. Hot dogs or hamburgers. I think she understands now why he wants to fatten her up. Because after a few bites she wants to gag. That's okay. I tell her that's fine. Even if vomiting seems to bother her. And the food she gets seems to be too much anyway. No matter how much I try, I cannot seem to make that new body disappear. Sometimes they even make it parade around. Like the models in the Miss Universe pageant. Though those at least get bathing suits.

The wallpaper hasn't been as effective as I thought it might be. I can already hear her start to whine. Deep in her throat it starts. EEEEEYEEE, EEEEEEYEEEE, EEEEEEY-EEE, like a hurt animal, that kitten of hers when it died of distemper, more than like a baby. It's that question coming up again. That question. The one I won't let her ask. Why me? she wants to say, Why me? But I won't let her. Isn't this fun? they'll answer. That's all they ever say. Because you're there, is what I whisper at her when she gets the question out, or tries to. Because you're there. Like that story about climbing mountains. I know about that, too. I'm far more sophisticated than she is. It's because you're there, I say. Because you're there. But no matter how many times I tell her, even when I scream at her late at night, I can't make her leave. She's stubborn that one. Stubborn. And pitiful really. She just doesn't get it. She won't disappear.

Or stop trying to ask her questions. She's really quite something once she gets going. All that, Why me? Followed by what did I do, followed by what did I do wrong, followed by did I eat too much of his ice cream, is it that I'm better in school, did I visit him too often late at night when people were drinking in the house, is it that I'm a better shot with his bow, did I need someone to talk to, is it that I lay down next to him, did I look at him pissing in the bathroom did I look at the sex manuals with him did I masturbate in front of the TV did I tell him about the boys at the school with their drawings of naked women did I try to draw a penis for him did he watch me do it did his friends watch me do it do I look different what is this body have his friends been watching have they been watching did they watch me did they see me did they see how bad I am. How bad I am how bad I am and her fingers will open and close and sometimes her nails will dig into her palms and she will tear at her arms and at her hips and they will notice her and make her do things until she will start to whine again. EEEEYEEE EEEEEEEYEEEE EEEEEEEEYEEEE that terrible whine as she rocks back and forth to cover her shame to cover her fear to try to throw it up and out only that doesn't work either. Even when she throws up so little comes out that it can't help her disappear, no matter what I do, I've discovered that.

I've got to start working on something else, some kind of new technique. So I start by telling her it's going to be all right. I don't even mention that stuff about how it's because she's there I just tell her it's all right. It gets harder and harder for her to take if you're not gentle with her, sometimes she starts to shake and to cry if you're not careful so I have to be very careful, very very careful, because if she does those things something worse will happen, I'm sure of it, they'll tie her up or make her do that thing with his prick again, it's not at all like the one she drew, not really, it's so thick and dry and it smells like pee when she puts it in her mouth even if they promise he won't pee in there still that would give her a real reason to gag just the way she did the last time when she cried too, great big tears, and she snivelled and she had to promise she would do anything they wanted if they just didn't make her do that, so I can't even warn her. Much less make her remember. If I remind her how much worse it might get if she doesn't pretend to go along she might panic, you can see how that's starting to happen anyway, it's not just the cold anymore, not at all, do you notice how her stomach is starting to heave her diaphragm is going into spasm, right there below those breasts I don't want to look at, only they do, god, the nipples are shaking and they're starting to look up, the two sets of eyes are going up and over, away from his prick for a moment, back over to her, so that I send her eyes once more up to the ceiling, Shshsh I say this time Shshshsh, calming the spasm and wishing their eyes away, They won't hurt you, really they won't, they won't hurt you, you'll see, I say, It will be all right, really it will, only I can't get close enough to reach out to her, not from where I am across the room, I have to stay here far away from her so they won't notice me, they won't notice where I've gone. Or how I try to help her.

I've noticed how she likes the colours that go off behind her eyes like silent fireworks when she squeezes them shut late at night when I make the cookies moulder and the voices to whisper, Get out. While she pulls her blankets up around her chin and screams back, I won't go I won't, she doesn't believe me when I tell her it would be better that way, sometimes she screams, This is my place so loud that someone comes running up the stairs to see her, times the music isn't too loud for them to hear. Even her brother comes sometimes, to comfort her. There, there, they say, there, there, it's going to be all right. She really likes that, that's where I got it from. Then they tell her it's only a nightmare, a bad dream, that she has a fever again, that she's anemic, catching too many colds, You have to promise to eat more, they say, sometimes they even hug her. Then they go away. Leaving the light on.

Mostly I don't scream at her then. Though I can choose to make the cookies and the cakes and the other food and even bodies disintegrate in the grey space in her mind if I really want to. Until she comes to prefer the dark. Times like this in the chair, she longs for it. With its colours, dark blue and purple inching into the grey ground, then yellow paisley and orange squares and red detonations. Like falling stars or northern lights. So that's what I'll give her. I've been working on this one a long time. It's going to be good. It'll work. Better than punishment. Better than screaming at her. Or even warning her. Better than starving her. You'll see.

I got the idea from how they tried to warn her once, too. When they took one of her dolls and tore it apart. Dismembered it and put its arms and legs in different parts of her chest of drawers, with the body hung in her closet. This could happen to you, they wrote on its chest. This could happen to you. They meant if she wasn't good. Or if she told. Only she has been good. And I will make sure she never tells. I will dismember her myself now that I know she can't disappear. But this won't be like what they did. It's not a warning. I'm going to make something beautiful. A blanket. I will make her a blanket. A blue and purple blanket. Fluffy, like the clothes in the drawer where she found the arms and legs. Even if it will have much less substance, still it will be of just the colours she might see if I could let her close her eyes. The ones she likes so much. So that while she watches them I can close her mind instead. Into silence.

Into this long tunnel where she cannot be hurt, where that blanket will cover her even as she sits in her chair. So that only the limbs, a foot or a hand, dirty with its broken nails and cut fingers, a nose or an eye or that piece of her rib cage, the line of stretch marks already present along her widening hips, might occasionally surface, just like the limbs did in the drawer. Only they will never be able to come together to reconnect that body, not even to find all its parts, the way the spots of paint led her to the limbless headless torso in the closet, with its sign and its hole, cut down there where that doll had never been meant to have one.

And there won't be any sentences either, to reconnect her to the body of her questions, to lead her back to her place of shame. But only words, occasional stray words, in many sparkling colours, like graffiti, lost and unconnected as they rise up in the space of that same covering blanket, bright like the shimmering of the stars behind her eyes, and all those words will be mine. And what will come out of that mouth that will appear too at the blanket's edge, just as the doll's mouth did among her underwear, will be the small short sentences I tell her to repeat again and again. Again. And again.

Who cares who cares who cares she will say now, who cares who cares who cares, what difference does it make anyway, while they just smile and go about their business, with their pricks or with their lives. And it will be just like cowboys and Indians, just like war, just like cops and robbers, just like terrorists and CIA agents, just like doctor and nurse, just like house. Her unremembered body over there just like any other toy, any other doll. Only it will be wrapped in this purple and blue, this multicoloured blanket of dismemberment, that will be forever empty of syntax and of emotion. A beautiful blanket so that I will never have to listen to her whine, or feel her shame. Not ever again.

There is only one problem. It is thirty years later. And I find myself putting my hand into my mouth, gagging on my food. While, seated in her chair, so long after the others have left, she still cannot get warm.

WITNESS

In some ways, of course, it will not start like this at all. This whole process. This journey. This quest. On which at first, this much is true, you will unknowingly embark. It will be completely different, both more fragmented and more difficult. The pain undisguised. Compelling you to fiction, to a daily kindness in small observations, written day after day, or to a cathartic writing down of stories, starting from a hallucinated sentence, something you actually hear, as if it were in the room with you. Something you cannot stand to have undefined one moment longer.

And, of course. It will not all be unremembered. Not unremembered at all. Just unrecalled, unorganized, abandoned, dismembered, torn apart, set adrift. Specific things, always deemed unimportant, hardly central to you, even if they would push you when first they came up, into a place where you could not speak.

And then there is how you will wake up night after

night, your body curled up, a gag — you can feel it — in your mouth. And all your organs in the wrong place. In their child place, at five, six, ten, twelve. The incidents not of remembered pain, the way we say in observation, Yes, that hurt, and then put whatever it was back away, but of pain recalled into the body. You will feel it, taste it, smell it, with always the laughter behind. And the only relief will be the knowledge of where you are, that this has been superimposed on you. And your greatest fear: That this knowledge will be taken, and you will be in that place forever. So that in the end, all of it — the fragments, the stories, the images, the incoherent ululation that seems to be there always in your mind if you just turn your ear inward — all of it will become simply a house, a dwelling, standing there halfway up the block like the one you grew up in. One you will stand outside, saying No, no, I do not wish to enter. No. No matter how often the door swings open.

You will enter it anyway. Compelled not by curiosity but by pain.

And the need, somehow to not say I, to see yourself as separate, a child, an adult, someone you can address and guide, tell what to do, or what will happen. As you move her into the future. Or someone you can separate completely, a she, a third person, someone you do not know. Who will create spin-offs of the self, those small fictions that are still truths.

And then, somewhere in here, in this widening spiral of revelations, when most of the terrible work of memory is done, but not the healing, you think sometimes that will never end, a close friend will come, to reveal to you yet something more, of who you have been. She will be your grade school best friend, from that time when having a best friend was the most important thing in the world. And she will be giving a lecture at the Glenbow Museum, about the Goddess, which only later will seem significant. As it will seem significant that this is the first piece you will feel compelled to write, when the other work is almost done, and you are simply gathering this into book form. So that, as she sits in front of you, at the restaurant, what will seem important is how she explains you to yourself, brings into focus your need to do this.

Not your need to follow out the traces of your pain, the particles in the cloud chamber of yourself. But your need to write it, to place your voices on the page, and finally to publish them. As you will look around the restaurant, the kind you always find in first-rate hotels, like the ones where you might be put up on a reading tour, the way the Glenbow now deals with Margot.

Before she arrives you will look around. Think, how inadequate, how awkward, you used to feel in places like this, so like the ones you would go to when your aunt and uncle were in town, or your mother was invited home to her own middle class family she had fallen down and away from, or the times you would still go to Manhattan after Mark Murphy's death, you thought he was your father then, to visit his few old friends from better times. And you will try to breathe, and looking at the linen on the table hearing the voices tinkling around you, for the first time in years have to fight to feel you belong here. That you will not do something terrible. Or that someone, catching a glimpse of you, will not come and ask you to leave. As Margot tells her story. Tells your story. Tells her story of you. Your story back to you. One you remember very well.

It will not be of the bright side of the childhood you shared, those special moments held in common that rescued you from the bleakness — how you became blood sisters in Central Park, underneath the castle-like weather station, up on the outcropping of Manhattan schist, New York's glinting bedrock, that overlooks the lake, so good for games of Amazons and goddesses and fantasy quests. Where you would visit always tucked into its tiny cranny, the bright penny of your pledge to each other, choosing according to the day and your confidence, to climb the rocks or walk out into the mud. Perhaps where you get your love of rock climbing from, that love of glancing up, calculating the route and the grips. Because it was you who always led the way, proud of your eye, the way you still are, for the little ledges onto which you can always tuck feet or hands, grab around, and keep moving. The way you were always the climber, that first love of your childhood, trees and rocks, the fronts of buildings, the girders of construction sites or bridges, laughing at heights, somehow freed by them the way you might now lean out over the edge of a cliff to look down at the stream below. Or enjoy rappelling down its face.

Though now, it's true, you will spend much more time looking, the way you look across at her, over the cliff of her eyes and a long way down into the story she tells. As you both gaze out from the contentment of your middle-aged bodies and the clarity of the present day into the turbulent and murky waters of the past, their grey swirling, the grey you have entered and not yet passed out of, as listening to her speak this time you will think, still feeling awkward, still the outsider: Why am I always the example in someone else's exemplary tale?

It won't just be the story she is telling. Or even the stories she now repeats that her mother told her, a beautiful, almost hysterically energetic, teacher and actress and long-time member of the Jewish left, a woman with tight curled hair who tanned so dark that, once mistaken for a black in the south, when the store owners addressed each other in Yiddish to say that one of her kind could be charged anything, she responded in Yiddish. And told them what she thought.

While you, I would guess looking back, you, were probably the nearest example of poverty as could be found to hand, to be made to exemplify some particular kind of difficulty, or at least Mickey would. A story familiar enough from the art world: What it means to fall down, what it means to never be picked up, or be able to pick yourself up, or your children. Telling Margot how she remembered you, coming into school, with a light jacket and no winter boots on the coldest snowy days, literally a snot-nosed kid. What you remember too: The snot permanently caked between and below your nostrils. You even thought it was natural, that it grew there. And on your feet just shoes. Old beaten up shoes, but a good brand because your aunt had bought them long before, brown and white or blue and white saddle shoes with old cotton socks. And newspapers used to line them.

Looking at Margot you will smile warmly and say, Oh, yes, that's right, I don't really remember but Bill must have done that. Then responding to her quizzical look, you will say, You know, Cherokee.

Your smile will grow wider as you think for the first time in a while about how you always called him that, how everybody did, that half-blood Choctaw always called by the name of another nation, the Cherokee. The largest, and perhaps the best organized, of the five nations moved to Oklahoma in the 1830s, the last to consent to removal, whose walk across the United States from the eastern seaboard was named the Trail of Tears. Something Bill will correct you on when you dedicate a book to him, using those words, as many do, to designate all the removals of the Five Tribes. While you still know, when he says, but all removals were bad, that the same portion died, one quarter, on the Choctaw walk from the Mississippi valley. Perhaps shame motivated him: the Choctaw had signed the treaties too soon, had believed the White Man, that Oklahoma would be forever Indian Territory, what the name says — Choctaw for Red People's Land.

You will think about this, your eyes wandering across the

carts full of fruit and waffles and whipped cream, while Margot looks on. Always going back to the question of who Cherokee Bill has been in your life, this man on whose shoulders you rode, laughing and wrestling, while your brother Tim rode on Mark Murphy's. Bill, the sailor who left for the darkest period of your life, the one whose features and whose length you cannot remember, only to come back to put Mickey's house in order. The one you have called by times, your mother's boyfriend, her lover, your stepfather, and finally your Dad. But this won't have happened yet. That Cherokee Bill will tell you he believes himself to be your father. In letters, and then in person, as you walk with him around Downeast Maine, and everyone tells you of the resemblance. A resemblance — so clear — that you will see only later as you accept this as fact, not from evidence — though there will be ample evidence, in Mickey's archives, in letters he had written you — but simply because he raised you, and loved you, and he claimed you, and he left you his legacy, and there is little more we can ask of our parents. Though this is a long time in the future still, and now, with Margot, what you will be thinking of is shoes. And it is only when you look back at her that you realize — again — how different your worlds are. The shock, the recoil on her face, tells you she doesn't understand. How come you are smiling like that. Why you could say those words with appreciation. What that could mean. It is almost as if you can see her thoughts in a bubble over her head. How could he, they read, how could he do that to you?

You laugh then. It's really very simple. Bill is the one who would have known. And coming into port and seeing that you had no boots, that in the chaos of your mother's alcoholic house she had been unable to supply you with boots, then newspaper at least was warm, the way those who have been truly poor, all over the world know that newspaper, that any old bulk paper, at least is warm, and absorbent, the way the homeless will still sleep with newspaper lining their shirts. The way you have too in moments of desperation when you were running away, the way, perhaps, Mark Murphy learned before he died. With Bill, of course, walking those miles to the reservation school — for once it will be true, that parental admonition — sometimes with no shoes at all, or sleeping out when he had to on the street, knowing as well as any what will work when survival is at stake and push comes to shove. When it is a question of elegance versus frostbite. Or death by exposure.

You will think how you owe him that, warm feet. Just as you owe him warm meals: Okra and rice and beans and *cafe con leche* and *chile con carne* northern style, from the California-Mexico border where he had lived with Yaqui cousins, that sometimes he made so hot even he couldn't eat it. And always in the brief periods of organization in the house, there was practicality against pretence, that sometimes went so far as to hock antique silver flatware as well as last month's radio, to buy food as he prepared to go to sea again to buy them back. So that yes, it would be him. The one who would tuck in the newspaper and tell you about it, instead of making you try to act as if you just forgot your boots, and wore your good shoes, battered as they were, instead. Something in those days you might have tried your best to think.

You look at them in your mind. A concrete image. Remembering how that was, your blue and white or brown and white top-of-the-line Buster Browns, cracked and broken down, the heels bent in, the toes scuffed beyond polishing, the dirty broken laces, the layered holes in their soles, then newspaper tucked around your chapped ankles where your wet socks had inched their way down. And the old jackets too, and the holes in the jeans, and the dirty hands and face, and short unkempt hair. And how you never really cared. Not at first. Even if it made the other kids look at you strange, and made you fight a lot. Fighting was, after all, what you did best anyway. While the rest of the time you just played. Played and climbed. And lived in your own world. And hardly noticed being different at all. Or you didn't think you did.

While the tests you were subjected to told another story. Judged you psychotic. At least that's what your mother said. The school had taken a chance just letting you in. Those tests were so bad, you read so highly emotionally disturbed, the school destroyed them. As soon as you improved. When they were no longer thinking of getting rid of you. It was the McCarthy era, after all.

It will be a long time before you notice what it cost you. Mostly, like Margot, you will tell chipper upbeat stories about what it was like to be on scholarship to that special progressive school. And maybe, mostly, they will be true. Certainly you felt safe there. But sometimes it will all come pouring out. What you felt you had to do to preserve that safety among the children of well-to-do intellectuals and leftists where they would do something like that. Destroy your tests because of how, in some unknown way, bad you were, so bad that those tests could somehow incriminate you in later life, the way they might have, the way you worry still. Not so much for you, not anymore, but for others, reading the headlines in *The Calgary Herald*, about a six-year-old girl sent to live with a grandmother who was known, besides living in a sexual relationship with her brother, to have abused the girl, and how now, after the problem has been noted, and the girl's been taken into foster care, the child's become "so sexualized she can't be allowed to play with other children," but must be institutionalized. While you wonder, no matter how often the papers reiterate that they cannot print her name for her own protection, how that story will follow her. Someone turning to her and saying, Well, you know what the newspapers used to say about you. And it still being her stigma, no matter what we say.

Though you, at approximately the same age, you don't know about her, were also said to be very very bright — perhaps brilliant. That's what the school said. That's why they took you. Something you were told again and again until you knew it was your bargaining chip. You will try to explain this, not to Margot but to another friend, a young Metis woman. Telling her about all those people with all their money and their radical convictions, and how you tried to imitate them, or at the very least imitate the deserving poor — those they thought of as the deserving poor, always trying to pass, thinking that if you did it hard enough you would become like them. And not just get away from the poverty, not even mostly from the poverty, all those nights with no food in the house, but from all the edges of terrible danger, the nights waiting to see who your mother would bring home and what she or they would do when she did — all that, the death and the fear of death, would go away. While your friend will look at you, ironic, and say, But how do you imitate boots — It must be damn hard to imitate boots.

You will feel suddenly exhausted, thinking of the energy it takes to shift shape, or create an illusion that all can see. You can feel it in yourself still, often enough, dressing or getting ready to teach or go to a reading, the draining of your energy to maintain the illusion. The illusion of boots, of boots like everyone else's boots. Willing the world to accept you with each waking breath, sometimes even in your dreams. And never thinking it has. As on your feet, in your mind, you remove the newspaper and create your boots anew.

With a sudden, if horrific, sympathy for Imelda Marcos and her two thousand pairs of shoes. The way your mother bought shoes, the minute the renovated house brought her money enough. So that she will die possessing easily a hundred pairs, along with the jackets, raw silk, smooth silk, shot silk, each in at least a dozen colours. While she would explain again and again, perhaps trying on a lime green sandal, how the heel broke off of her last pair of good high heels — the ones she needed to job hunt in Manhattan — the night she went to Montero's Bar and Grill and Bill was there after those years sailing out of other ports, a symbol for her both of hitting the skids, and of last-minute rescue. Though she would never stay rescued for long.

It will be easy for you to understand certain forms of greed and corruption. As you think of what it means to imitate being yourself in order to be like them. Just the exact right poor person for your place and time. The one someone will inevitably offer to take away from all that. Or at least home to dinner. You will know too, when you hear that comment, what it was, the sudden exhaustion, the feeling that your body is coming apart at the seams, its joints parting, as you spoke with Margot. As you will think again of that image she has presented of those beaten up saddle shoes, as specific as anything could ever be, and you will see a lifetime spent trying to imitate boots. Even as you will find your mind still whispering to you: I don't always want to be the moral in someone else's morality tale.

You will notice that Margot has continued on to another story. Not her mother's, but her own. One you both share and which you will remember well. After all, you tell it often enough yourself, even if in abbreviated form. To make it part of the childhood you have always allowed yourself to have in public, talking about being what is still called a tomboy, a tomboy and proud of it, you would often say, and describe how you would often fight, and often win, and sometimes fight dirty, though only when ganged up on. When sometimes you lost, though seldom badly. As you might go on, turning from that to talk of your love of climbing, how later, much later with your girl gang you formed the Ginkgo Club.

Of which Margot was an honourary member since she seldom made it to Brooklyn, though she too loved that tree in your backyard with its dusty green fan-shaped leaves.

In talking you will make yourself forget what that word could mean, the badly of the seldom badly, how bad that could be, no matter how seldom, that losing when it happened. The desperate sobbing after a bunch of neighbourhood boys caught you, and stuck a cigarette butt up in there, the way you always thought of it, an in there or up there you didn't hardly acknowledge, caught that day inside one of the stoops behind a little wrought iron door, once the servants' entrance, where garbage cans or brooms were mostly kept, and the gang of boys spreading your legs, and you learning what it is to sob without stopping. Even if later, you would find them. And beat them up one by one. While too, there was this story. Perhaps not so very bad, perhaps worse. But the one Margot tells you.

The quintessential playground story, really. Though, traditionally, it is the one for the boys. The women's equivalent seems to be The Makeover, when the kid who doesn't fit in is finally outfitted and made up by someone who does, someone who can see the beauty beneath the appearance and bring it out so that the misfit is suddenly and miraculously attractive. And everyone understands the ugly duckling is now a respectable swan. With this one, The Fight. The one that is always there, told and retold. The one that proves somehow that it's not whether you win or lose but how you play the game. The one where the new kid, the misfit — the poor kid, the rich kid, the black kid, the Irish kid, the one with glasses or a limp — any difference will do you, the one who can't get along, or just doesn't, has his moment of truth. To learn who he really is. Or who he can be. Whatever shape it is he's in when the fight is over. Or, if he is too bad off, too much a misfit, a permanent outsider, someone else learns. Of compassion. Or morality. Watching him. What you feel now:

I don't want to be the moral in someone else's morality tale, a voice repeats.

Because in this case, it was a she. And it was you. And it was true. All those typical facts about the new kid were true. Your case the most typical — or stereotypical — of all, with the torn clothes and the dirty hair, only your sex at variance. And really, nobody had wanted to talk to you, and you hadn't wanted to talk to anybody, and everyone hated you and you knew it. They made fun of you and called you names, while you in vengeance, you ruined their games, or started a fight, or just sat on the bottom of the slide. So that if anyone slid down and bumped into you while doing it, the fight would start then, and you would even feel justified. After all, you had been there first, and you didn't care, how long you had been there, or if it was the best use or not of the slide, or if it ruined someone's fun, yours had been ruined often enough, and this was a territory you could claim and fight for. So that you just sat there. Beneath their noses. Beneath their notice. Or just their feet. In the exact place where they would have to notice you.

Only on this particular day, the fight wasn't over the slide. You had been in a different yard from the slide — there were three of them in that school — and the slide was in the Block Yard, where there were giant building blocks of plywood and even bigger boxes, and boards of green-painted one-by-six, so you could build forts the way you did in the classrooms out of plain wood blocks. Except that these you could go inside and walk between, the way you did between the two buildings of the school, which was made really of two Greenwich Village townhouses and the yards between. So that the other two yards were the Big Yard, which was paved and used for organized sports and games, dodge ball or soccer or even baseball, it did have a diamond painted on it, but it took up the whole rectangle from one end to the other, there was no outfield, and it was covered with a net you always wanted to climb into, as well as onto the fire escape the way you did at home, only you weren't allowed except for the day of the fair.

And as for baseball, you could outrun everybody, and catch too, but you could never learn to hit or throw, so you were always picked last for the team even when things got better, though the same wasn't true in soccer or dodge ball. While the third yard, right next to the covered but unheated passage that went from building to building was a long rectangle called the River Yard. Because at one time, they said, a river, whose name you've forgotten, but which began with 'M' and was definitely Iroquois, had run through it before it was buried. Bottled and buried, run through a tube, the way rivers inside cities often are, until it could only be seen at one local hotel, to which field trips were organized — you are sure of that — where a spring from the river was allowed to well up in the lobby before it was sunk again.

The River Yard had a tire swing, and some other playground play thing at its other end, you've forgotten what, and was gravel-covered like the Big Yard, and was a good place to go when you wanted to be alone, because there were no blocks there and no one built castles or played hide and seek, or any other game they could leave you out of, so you would just go in there sometimes, and swing and swing, and your dirty underwear would show through the holes in your jeans and you just wouldn't care. Only there might come a time in the play period, when all the other kids, or at least some, would want too, to play on the swing. When maybe you would have it already staked out. It was yours. They hadn't let you in on the games they were playing, and you weren't going to let them have their turns on the swing. So you would fight the others off when they came to take it from you. As often as not, kicking out with your legs as you just kept on swinging.

While on this day, after the first two or three kids went off crying and complaining, a gang was organized to get you off the swing. Which they did. Flooding in from the Block Yard waving the six-foot-long one-by-sixes, they hit at you with them even as you swung away and tried to kick out. Until all of them, six or seven, eight or ten, you can't remember, but all the boys in the class that day, came in to tear at you, and to pull you off the swing. While you still fought back, fists and feet swinging, bringing one of them to the ground with you, and then another, as they screamed and called you a dirty fighter, as you started to scratch and even to bite, before they finally pinned you down, and then taking arms and legs hauled you off, dragging you along the ground through the concrete hallway and into the Block Yard, pulling down your pants, laughing, as your underwear came down with them. So that you were dragged, half naked and screaming, along the gravel, until you were deposited, your pants down around your ankles, in front of the girls in the Block Yard. Where they all proceeded to look at you and call you names and laugh. And that is what Margot will remember.

How she stood there.

And although she remembers it all as taking place in the River Yard by the tire, and you remember being dragged, still it is the same: how you were stripped and how she stood there. And how she deeply knew at the age of seven that this was wrong. What was being done to you was wrong. Yet she stood there. Knowing equally well, even as her tongue worked in her mouth, trying to speak, that she did not want the same thing to happen to her. As she knew that it would. If she came to your defence. So that she stood there. And knew the raw feeling in the throat, the horror, of what it is to not be able to bring yourself to stand up for what you know is right. And even to know that doing so would make no difference anyway. The way people do sometimes, you have seen this, when one victim is singled out for a beating or death or torture, by a mob, or by the police. So that any gesture from her, would just have given this baby mob another, though more respected, victim. Which meant that all she could do was watch carefully and let it engrave itself on her mind, the exact actions of what they did to you. While she just grew colder, knowing how wrong it was.

You will know too — it is why she speaks — that, in the way of such playground morality tales, this moment altered the course of her life. That something in watching you being dragged naked across the gravel set the underground river of herself along a course that would always be the same, the knowledge given her that moment bringing her to the bearing of witness, the saying what you see, that has defined her. Just as later, your two lives would intertwine playing Amazons and goddesses by that rock in Central Park together. While you will know too, how that moment changed the course of your life, the life of that child you sometimes call Jane, trying to find a tenderness for her. Who, too, was changed forever.

That is not what you will think of now. Instead there is that other roaring underground current, the one that you have not listened to in years. The one that connects you to that defiant child sitting on the bottom of that slide, singing and humming, *Kevin Barry* and *La Cucaracha*, the only two songs she knows, swinging on that tire. The one who refused them. Who would imitate neither boots nor words, who was angry and ugly and herself, the one you can hear now, howling at you, not a song, but words: I want my story, mine. Harsh and whining. I want to tell it. The child you have been hearing and rephrasing, ever so polite: I do not want to be the moral in someone else's morality tale, the example in someone else's exemplary tale, I am not part of a book of examples.

You can still hear that voice. Still feel it. Fierce. Enduring. Suspicious. I do not want to be Margaret Laurence's Piquette, the voice says, sitting opposite the protagonist in the café, in that café, or in this restaurant, about to disappear forever into the fire. You can even hear the children in the neighbourhood howling at you, Ooh wah wah ooh wah wah, such a different ooh wah, their hands cupped and uncupped over their mouths, them the cowboys and you, with your Dad — whether or not you knew he was your father — still making you, not the Indian but the half-breed. And behind that howling that other voice, not your own, but the voice of that child you left behind to become Margot's friend and imitate boots — imitate yourself — insistent now. I don't want to be the moral in someone else's morality tale. One of those always other, always somehow at least slightly lower-class children, vaguely dirty vaguely wrong, snot-nosed and just too badly dressed to take home to dinner, who sets those middle-class kids on their path of moral rectitude. Who makes them incapable of torture, or insider trading, or joining the CIA, or acts of overt racism. Who teaches them that indeed, the other, any other, is as human as they are. Who makes them clamour for justice, even if they know as well as the unconverted others of their class who surround them, that such justice is, at least temporarily, unavailable. And that they benefit from its lack. So that they are turned to quixotic acts of bravery and of witness. Often enough between glasses of champagne and orange juice and *The New York Times* or at least a cappuccino on Sunday mornings.

While you, that child you, that other you, is as soon dropped from the story. Once the lesson is learned. The words for it honed, polished. After all, one really doesn't want her around. She'll do something disgraceful later, steal a silver spoon or break a long-stemmed wine glass, or read Harlequin Romances, or call someone a Wop, or just not understand the question. Turning around to challenge the morality so nicely learned by being herself — and, you know, just so unremittingly, well, how can we put it, lower class.

You will feel the crying out, her crying out, that small child, those small children, the one, the ones, you have come by then to call Jane, their voices speaking out in your mind, speaking into your mind, the way you have been listening to them, by the time you see Margot, for years. Jane for the most common of ordinary names, Jane for the child who is any child and yet not any child at all, but the outcast. Jane for her commonness, and too, for her voices. For an early identification with Joan of Arc, from that same summer before you went to that school, or the summer before, when Paul Garcia, your Mexican stepfather, your mother's Sonoran lover, took you into a barbershop in your blue jeans and the man gave you a crewcut, when all you could think of was that other Jane, Joan or Jeanne — Jean Seberg you are almost sure, Ingrid Bergman's hair was far too long and resembled yours when it was grown out, a golden cap, but not a crewcut, so that it must have been Jean Seberg. Jean Seberg as Joan of Arc. Jeanne D'Arc. Jane Dark. Your Jane. Your Janes. Jane Dark. Out of the dark.

Looking at Margot you will remember all the voices coming out of the dark. The ones you have been hearing for so long now. And writing down. And taking in to your therapist. The ones that will finally pursue you out into that field of pain, you will find no other way of saying this, a simple metaphor, almost a cliché, it might seem, except it seems literal to you, deep red and featureless, something you cannot calculate, where you seem to wander, unable to find direction, even the way ghosts do in silly movies, to find a floor you won't sink through. Or a voice, any voice at all, to call you back. Where you will not be able to speak of any of this at all. Hardly hear words spoken to you.

You will remember too, the first time it happened. And the pain of that first voice. A day when you are sitting in your therapist's office, looking for the first time through the grey place into the split that has allowed you to become yourself. The place where Jane lives. Where she has been placed — you will not for the longest time know why, whether it is so that you can desert or protect her. You will only know that it has been so that you could leave — to become other, whether in flight or quest you do not know — that place, where over the months, more and more, you will conclude, with guilt or shame or just relief, she still lives. Only on that day, you will not yet have looked at any of this, as you look first at your therapist's feet and then at your own, and then fail to comprehend the distance between them, until the space between you twists and becomes powdery, a void, distorted, absolute, uncrossable. When you find yourself looking at your hands for comfort, the details of the lines and of the scars around your knuckles, fixing yourself there, as you realize you cannot do it. Answer his one question.

What was it that happened with your brother? he will have said. Or he may have used the word exactly. Exactly what was it that happened with your brother? Because you have mentioned it before, a kind of code. This, because of what happened with my brother. That, because of what happened with my brother. My older son, I cannot deal with his adolescence, because of what happened with my brother. Coded, filed away somewhere, this and always this, will be remembered, despite what else is forgotten.

Yet somehow unimportant, even if it made you bad. You knew by the time this happened that you could fool the world into thinking you good. And manifestations of badness had to be put away. Though you had learned this by then, you were what, eleven, twelve: That you needed the information to remember yourself. Even if there were other things that you sheltered in those blue parentheses you will become used to seeing. Like flags in the mind. Black holes into which the self is poured. Along with all emotion. Going beyond bad to the edge of dissolution. But out of which the voices come, from those selves, those Janes, who, you will discover over the months to come, in the months before you see Margot, were the selves you preferred to forget. And the enormous blue-red gap that has always been there, years of it, before you met Margot the first time, surrounding that time between Cherokee Bill's leaving and his return, when Mark Murphy, the man whose name you bear, the one you thought so long your father, the *New Yorker* writer, took a last assignment and went to South Africa to die. The years that ended with you being judged a psychotic child, and your tests destroyed.

Except that now, now, once you have mentioned your brother to your therapist — and you won't know why this should be, what particular ability you are giving him to validate you — you find you cannot remember the emotion and remain yourself. That to tell it in that room you must tell it — not as that thing you flick off, a hand gesture to the side, as childhood sex-play — but as it felt. And you can't do that. And leave your world in place. The grey, the dark, starts to spark with colour, and to creep up to dissolve even the edges of your fingers, until you cannot imagine yourself moving, even as far as the door. But sink deeper and deeper into that immobilizing space. Until you are unaware of what causes it. Even of your pain.

Until finally you will say: I don't think I want to answer that question. Because it is the only answer you can give, that you know will break the spell. To get you safely out the door. The only words that will give you the door's location. In the far wall. So that getting up slowly you can move through it.

When you get home you will find that it has not been so simple. The question remains. And you find that, shaking, you must answer. Even if your therapist has said you do not have to, that you can go on without doing that, still, you know you must. And you do. Beginning. Just like that: I will answer your question if you really want me to. Even if it is really you who craves the answer. Even if it is really a voice that is both you and not you, who answers it. The first voice. Of many.

The next week you will take the writing in, and leave it with him, because you cannot speak. Not of that. Or only coming at it, from some strange, oblique angle. To begin months, even years, where you will feel something caught in your throat, as the voices speak in your mind. You, so easy to words, finding them so hard. To get them off your tongue. Even as within weeks you will hear the next voice, from a little girl, standing on the top floor of your mother's house, near the stairwell. I will never tell, she says, and then you hear the words of your balancing act, being spoken. Before even writing is lost, in that space where over and over your speaking voice has been silenced by the amorphous grey, the dark. That you cannot get Jane Dark out of. Until finally you will have to go back to coloured chalks to draw yourself a pathway.

You will think of this process again as you look at Margot. You have come such a long way. With the words easier now. Even as she tells you — before you mention any specifics — that the only time in her life she came even close to feeling sexually abused was in your house, with your brother. Who learned it from his friend who learned it from his military school who learned it from — you can see it all echoing back down the lines of generations and experience, with both of them too young to know, and your house, with the other more terrifying abuse in it, too dislocated to teach them. But it is not this you will think about.

Though it will take time to go through it again. Complete the circle you will have to complete over and over throughout your therapy, going from blaming yourself that this could happen to Margot, to understanding it was not your fault, it was not you who did it. And still you will spend your time, for a while, sunken in that shame. Thinking that somehow she was contaminated by knowing you, the way you will feel off and on the world has been contaminated by knowing you.

You will know too, that you must do it. As you look at Margot and Jane cries out again. Overcome that shame once and for all. Take up at least that one aspect of yourself. Say clearly who you are. That she is you. Even as that other voice says again: I do not want to be the example in someone else's exemplary tale.

This time it is up to you to let her tell it. You must let Jane tell it. Just the way she tells you to. Repeating: It is my story, mine. This time it is my turn, mine. You must let those voices who have spoken through your hands tell their stories onto the printed page. Be their own examples in your book of examples.

You will be sure it is right. That those stories, even those drawings — made as a private act of story and of witness between you and your therapist those months you could not speak — must be made public to tell the story that she, that you as a child, that this voice still in your mind, now wishes told. That truly this time you will tell it. And take Jane Dark out of the dark. You will not let her be the moral in someone else's morality tale. You be the example in someone else's exemplary tale. Not this time.

But, looking at Margot, you will also know something else. Something of equal importance. As you will think of this whole long road you have walked. Margot, sitting opposite you, never did cut you out of the story. Never did put you back away. But from that day forward, after looking at you being stripped and beaten across the playground, was never ashamed of you, even as you, going home that day, like many others, will be ashamed of yourself. But instead went out of her way to understand you, to become your friend. And not out of pity, or to understand how the other side lives. But in genuine, abiding friendship. That helped to form you both. That made you say, if you have one friend, it is enough. You know who you are.

You said it already by the end of that year, you have no idea where you got it from. But you even remember standing in the Block Yard before the slide saying it: If I have one friend, it is enough. I know who I am. As you prepared yourself, eight years old, to come back the next year. To a wonderful year that still — when you have been asked at professional development conferences for language teachers to visualize a good learning environment — is the one you see, before bursting into tears.

You will think too, of your therapist, of the hours he has spent in the small acts of witness to these stories, the questions he has asked, to bring you forward out of the dark. The gestures made to you, by him, and by those closest to you. When you did not know if you would make it through this at all. And how there are still times, shorter now, when the grey darkness is such that you are not yet sure you have. When again, he will witness you. Or Tom will. Or Leila. Who have witnessed you again editing this. To make you think again of how important it is, that act of witness. That goes so far beyond the mere observation, of the hack journalist, or all the other tourists of alien pain. The way Margaret Laurence always went beyond. So that if Margaret Laurence saw Piquette, it was important that Margaret Laurence speak Piquette. That always, as best we can, we must say what we see. And that we must try to see, truly see, not just look at briefly and put away, but see, as much as we can. That it is from there, changing the story, by seeing it differently, we change the world. And years later you will think too, of Bill Sherar, your father. The man who has at last said this to you, clearly. Or, who you have, at last, heard speaking. That in Margaret Laurence's world, not the one she came from but the one she created, your mother too — among so many other things — would have been able to admit to him. Not just as lover, but as father to her daughter.

Yet still you will feel a cold in your feet and in your hands. The memory of the playground gravel on your bare body, digging into your thighs your buttocks your genitals. Other memories, too. Far more terrible. Coming with the dark winds of the hours spent trying to find and not finding your own voice. The hours spent in a pain so deep you did not think you could take another step. Or get up to move from where you were huddled in a corner. That will let you know that it is not always true that a friend can save you through giving you meaning, nor a witness validate your experience to bring you forward. When breathing deep you will feel the burning in your lungs, so cold it's hot, so hot it's cold, when you do not know if you are in danger of burning up or freezing.

You will think then of the fire. Piquette's fire and the fire that consumed the body of Joan of Arc, that has burned at the body of your Jane, and tempted you to burn her too, you and the children within you, the voices, trying to torment them into going away, only to hear just the laughing voices of your tormentors. As you would bring burning cigarettes into contact with your skin, cut through it with a razor, to rid yourself of it, the fire. And of her, the child on fire. So that sometimes you will think, sometimes. And know that it is true. It is the obvious truth behind the word survivor, that no one ever speaks: Not everyone survives. You have done so only barely — with great luck, and great help.

So that sometimes. Like the one who watches the mob and can do nothing. Who watches someone sink under the weight of her pain and can do nothing. The witness is the only survivor. The only survivor. Which makes it all that more important that we bear our witness well.

You will think too of your silence. That has been the child's silence. And of how you, too, have survived to witness her. That this was what she did not have the strength to do, when you split yourself to leave her behind. Your own wounded war-buddy buried in the window box in your mother's house. That you have allowed yourself to be the vehicle to witness her, to let her speak. So that as you think of your life, of how you have gone forward and the things you have done, you know that you, the you that now listens to her, are the moral in her morality tale. And she, who waits for you, and calls you back, the example in your exemplary tale. Each voice an example, in a book of examples. Yourself your own example. Of morality and — sometimes — of heroism.

So that thinking of that, and of how you must bring her forward, you will think too, of how hard it has been. How hard you know it will be again. No matter how much longer the good days are. So that you will become once more unsure of the results of your quest. Unsure of yourself, of Jane, even of your identity. At the same time as you tell yourself that without risk, there is no quest at all. And certainly no vision.

Still you will doubt how you will come to its end. If you will come to its end. Or if you will have a voice when you do so. So that as you take it up, once more, your quest, your journey, to find Jane Dark and bring her out of the dark, as you once more listen to her words, you will ask — I will ask — as the hero asks in the tales, for just this one small boon: If I do not make it to the end, dear reader, witness her.

Witness her.

Witness me.

BALANCING ACT

She's convinced it's her own fault, really. That's the truth. No matter what she says. All of it. She blames herself for all of it. The bad things that keep happening to her. She doesn't know why. But she thinks it's because she's curious. Even at the kindergarten they said she asks too many questions. About everything.

Getting her to do things used to be easy. Like taking candy from a baby. Or giving it in her case. She'd take anything she was offered. And she'd go anywhere you asked. She wanted everything. Hugs or kisses or answers to questions. Or even that play among the tangled sheets. With its kisses inside her mouth. Its hands along her body. When she was so easy to trap.

Now she doesn't want to be curious anymore. She's just scared. Scared all the time. Mostly scared except when she's angry. That's why I came to help her. Because they keep trapping her anyway. She doesn't know how to tell them to stop. To tell them it makes her feel bad. Maybe she's afraid they will go away altogether, the way they say her father did. Maybe she thinks that would be worse. Even if I'm here.

It's not so scary when she can talk to someone. When she has someone to play with. Who can take her mind off what's happening. We have our own kind of play. And a wonderful language. We whisper in it together. We have long conversations. And we write in it too. She's a good writer now. She makes beautiful titles for her pictures.

I can't help wishing she felt better, though. She says she used to. That her body felt good. That it didn't itch all over right under the skin, and that she enjoyed taking her clothes off. She says it felt good to have baths with her brother, and for someone to come and wash her. Even peeing in the tub felt good.

They both did that. And farted. So they could watch the bubbles. Though he did it more. Peeing out of his pee-nis, she used to say. Then one day she took his legs and whipped them up over his head while he was doing it and he peed in his face, and she ran away. All the way down the stairs laughing, while he peed over the banister after her. But she says that was fun. And that there was no harm in it.

It's not like that now. Even with her brother. I don't know what happened. Now she fights more than she runs and jumps. And she doesn't want anyone to bathe her. Or to touch her. And she doesn't like hugs and kisses unless she's really upset. And sometimes not even then. She just huddles in the back of her closet, and we talk. She's afraid they would notice something if they came too close. Then everyone would know what the ones who trap her know. Maybe then they would all make her do bad things.

So she's ashamed of everything. That time she got ringworm. She was sure she got it because she was bad. How bad I am, how bad I am, she whimpered to me. Then she told her mother she hadn't scratched any place, she hadn't touched them. There are no more, Mom, I haven't touched myself she said. She wanted to save herself the examination, especially inside her underwear. When she would close her eyes and whisper to me. Completely still. Like she was saying a prayer. Just the way she is when the bad things happen.

She had waited days before she told anyone, looking and looking in the mirror downstairs for hours, concentrating on the first one on her cheek, a red spot that she watched grow bigger and bigger. Until it became a ring. Then she tore at it. Because she knew they would see it then. And she was sure that circle on her face had come just to show the world what was wrong with her. That it was a secret brand that only the bad received. That everyone could read. And by then she had them all over. From all that scratching to make the first one go away. So she didn't even want to go out until they were gone.

Then when she got the sore inside her mouth, way back on her gum, she didn't tell anyone at all. She knew she didn't have to. She knew they couldn't see. And she didn't even care how bad it tasted. Or that it always felt so squishy when I touched it, as she let its liquid ooze out into her mouth. She thought she deserved that. Bad tastes for bad girls who do bad things.

She's the same way about going to the doctor. She always calls me to come help her when she goes. It's one of the times I get to go outside. When she points out the grass by the edge of the sidewalk, or the caterpillars. And I tell her how lovely they are. Sometimes we even sit down and rest. And I sing a little song in her ear. Or recite a poem. Help her play patty cake. The last time she lagged behind and got her shoe caught in the mud. She tried to look down into the pit where they're starting to build a new apartment building, while I balanced on the edge. Anything is better than thinking about the needle. Or even worse, the moment when the doctor will look down there, opening that place between her legs, to see if there's any white stuff, or any stains on her underwear.

It usually goes okay if she doesn't scream. Or moan and groan and throw herself around so that they have to hold her down. Or carry her while she yowls and kicks. That usually doesn't happen until she gets to the doctor's office. When she goes completely out of control. I just hope they don't take her back to that other doctor. The one who makes her play with blocks. And asks all those questions. She forgets that she was sick for a long time, and that she's gotten better.

Or how much fun it was to play on her bed, by ourselves, when no one else was around to bother her. Even if the medicine did make her dizzy. And me lose my balance. She thinks that the tests mean she will start to rot soon too. Just like my gum, she says. Just like those things I see at night. The ones you make me look at. And that's true, too.

Sometimes I do torment her. Sometimes I even agree that anyone who thinks she's so bad deserves to have bad things happen. That's what her brother's friend tells her. When you're bad you're bad. And everything else follows naturally. Except that he thinks he's bad. And the only bad thing that's happened to him is those glasses he has to wear. He's blind without them. The rest of them he just does. But I guess that makes you bad. It's funny that way.

Mostly I just do the things she asks me to. That are just like the things they do with her. The ones she wants them to do with me now. Like getting down under her mother's bed where we can see the old springs all covered with dust, while she plays with herself down between her legs the way they ask her to. Only when she does it herself she still tries to make herself feel good. She doesn't just pretend she isn't there.

Sometimes it does feel good for a while. Until her whole body seems to itch and hurt again and she wants to explode and tear at herself, and she imagines those things. The ones I torment her with later. Like seeing her body painted the way her mother's was after that operation, all red from belly button to halfway down her legs, when she watched her from the bed. Then she imagines herself pinched and prodded. While lots of people touch her. All dressed in white like doctors sometimes. Or she remembers the old cigarette butt being stuck up there between her legs.

Once she had me imagine she was being cut up, that the springs were twisting around her and trapping her and poking into her and opening her up and making her part of the bed. Only that went out of control. And it really scared her. Like the rotting sometimes does. When she really starts to scream. Then she thinks I do it on purpose. The way they do. That I enjoy seeing her like that.

She thinks it proves there's more wrong with me than there is with her. I don't think I believe that. Even if I don't remember being a baby the way she does. You know where babies come from but you don't know where you come from, she chants at me. But I still don't believe what she says. It's not true. That I just arrived one day. Just because she called me in that language we both speak. Or that I wasn't anywhere at all before I was here. I think she got me instead of the little sister her mother got rid of when she had that operation. I think I come from a circus. She found me in a circus. And brought me home. I think I was the tightrope walker.

She used to love to go to the circus with the one they call her father. I don't think I ever met him. Maybe I saw him at the circus once, but that's all. When they would sit way high up in the last rows. At the same level as the trapeze or those women who spin around on ropes by their teeth. Or the highest high wire acrobat. And she would laugh and clap. And insist on being bought one of those thin plastic kewpie dolls. Then she would go home and draw. All those women balanced in high and difficult places. And write underneath them, in letters just like the ones we use. In a language just like the one we speak.

That's why I think that's where I'm from. I must have been a baby tightrope walker. I must not remember. The way there are so many things that she does not remember. There must be things I forget, too. Like being a baby. Or having wonderful soft pillows, or towel rides along the floor. Or the circus. All those bright colours. And how I looked down onto the crowd.

I help her learn it all sometimes, though. Maybe that's why I was chosen to come here. To teach her those things. Because the tightrope act always was her favourite. So I help her do it. Even if we don't have a rope we have a fence in the backyard. Made of wire with metal tubing along the top. We can pretend the tubing is a rope. And I can help her balance. Walking along with her hands held out from her sides.

She does well most of the time. Even if there was the one time she fell. That was very bad. I started to think about one of those awful times and she noticed and she stopped paying attention and she fell. Just like that. And hit the concrete with her mouth.

She knocked out a tooth. That was the bad part. She said it was my fault. You see, you're the one, she said. You're the bad one. And she shut me up in the dark. Until I had to send her those awful visions again. They were perfect for when they gave her that gas and she saw all those colours. When they tried to put the tooth back in. Visions to make her remember how much she needs me.

It worked. She took me out of the dark so we could play together. And whisper in the closet. Only they made her think I was even badder. See the things you do, she said. See. I wasn't like this before you came along.

So now she makes me do all the bad things by myself. Circus people are good at that, she says. Standing around without any clothes. Or being touched all over. Circus people are good at that. They're pro-mis-cu-ous. And she writes it in the language we speak together. Though she never draws the bad things or says them out loud. I'll make you come out, if you mention any of it, she says.

Then she tells me it's all my fault. That's her favourite thing now. It's all your fault, she says. Then she tells me that she can make me come out if she wants. But that's just to scare me. And it doesn't anyway. That's not what I'm scared of. Not really. I just tell her that to reassure her when we go to that doctor. Don't make me come out. I'll never come out, I say. But it's really like Br'er Rabbit saying, Don't throw me in the briar patch.

I like it when I get to come out. As long as I don't have to talk to the others. When I can rest up in the corners of rooms. On lampshades or dusty chandeliers. I can try my balance on the mouldings, or slide down the wires the pictures hang from. And land on my feet with a bow. While I hardly notice what's going on around me. I just concentrate on my work. I'm good at all that. I'm a tightrope walker for sure. I know that now.

But it doesn't make me like the bad things. It doesn't even make me like to watch them. And they're not my fault. I didn't make her feel the way she does. And I don't make her scratch at herself or tear at her hair. Even try making cuts in her skin with knives. Little cuts where the ringworms were. I don't do that. And even if I helped her under the bed it was still her suggestion. She said she needed it. I prefer to climb trees. Or to walk on the fence.

She even threatens me about that now. Soon I'm going to be able to do it all by myself, she says. Then I won't need you. You can just keep doing all those bad things you like so much all by yourself, she says. You by yourself and me by myself, she sings.

And even when I say I don't want to, she just says, Shhhh, and goes back to hurting her dolls. And secretly doing to them the bad things she pretends not to remember. The ones she now says are all my fault. That's what really frightens me. That if she doesn't need me anymore she'll just shut me up in the dark except to do those bad things. And that's all I'll get to do. Bad things all by myself.

She seems to be able to do that. To keep me in here. Where there's no light at all. But I can't do it to her. All I can do is send her those visions. Or whisper in her mind. And then she blames it all on me. See how bad you are, she says. Even as she tears at her body. Or her dolls. See how bad.

Sometimes I think I really was a baby once. Sometimes I think I'm the one who went to the circus and had those baths. Sometimes I think that. Sometimes I think she's lying to me. She can't ever have liked that body she mistreats so much. That she's so ashamed of. But she just laughs. No, no, she says. This is your picture, she says. And she shows it to me on a piece of yellow paper. Here on the tightrope, with the umbrella. A little girl balanced on one foot. And she laughs. And we talk about the circus. And we're both happy.

Then suddenly she says, But I'm going to make you go away. And she takes a black crayon. And she rubs it all over my picture. Holding it in her closed fist. And then she tells me she's going to shut me in the dark. For a long long time, she says. Because of all those bad things I do. People who do bad things get shut in jail, she says. They get punished. They go where they can't tell their awful stories to anyone. And she laughs. And she presses harder with the crayon. Harder and harder. Sometimes I go away then. Sometimes she doesn't even have to tell me to.

She's almost as good at reading and at writing as she is on the fence now. I used to help her with that, too. But the last time they made her go see the doctor with the blocks she wouldn't even let me do that. She wants to write in that other language now. The one the doctor can read. To show off. It makes the doctor smile at her. And she wouldn't even let me play with the blocks.

I told her I wouldn't come out, no matter how many trick questions they asked. That's the point you know. You have to be careful with the questions. That you might answer,

Oh yes when I was in the circus. Or, When they put a cigarette butt up there, or something. Instead of how much you like your brother, and your mother's new boyfriend. You might say he's better than the last one who kicked her head open. So that you could see all the way into her brain.

I know she doesn't have to worry about me, even if I remember more about the bad things by now than she does. She doesn't have to shut me up to stop me from telling. Because I'm smart. I'll never come out. Not to where they can see me. And I'll never open my mouth. Even if I did perch up in the doctor's bun. And walked, balancing, along the tight wires of her hair. They never even knew I was there.

But she's different now. She's the one who's changed. She's determined to get into that special school. Determined to get all the answers right so they accept her. She even tries to stop fighting. To smile more. She thinks that if they do, it will be safe to be curious again. And maybe she won't have to do any more bad things. Or send me to do them.

You won't get to do what you like to do most, she says. Maybe you'll get to stay in the dark instead, she says. Maybe I'll meet other little girls, she says. Girls that aren't like you, she says. Who don't like bad things, she says.

I won't be able to let you meet them, you know. They'd think you were dirty. A dirty pro-mis-cu-ous circus person. So you'll have to stay shut up. Shut up, shut up shut up. Now it's your turn to shut up, to be shut up, shut up shut up, she says. And she giggles. And then she relents for a moment and takes me for a walk. And we talk to the ants and the ladybugs. And last week there was a praying mantis who spoke our language.

Sometimes when she's nice like that I still try to explain. To make her understand how unfair she is. That she can't just shut me up after all I've done for her. I start off quite casual. As if I were speaking about the weather. I didn't make you feel this way, you know, I try to whisper. I didn't do it.

I didn't feel ashamed of getting ringworm from petting a cat, I say. And I didn't want you to feel that way either, I add, to help make it better.

But she just pretends she doesn't hear. And she sings a little song. Rot in hell, if you tell, something like that. Something I didn't teach her. And then when I try to scream over the noise, she just sticks her fingers in her ears.

I do wish she would listen. She should remember who did this to her. She should. Who made her feel this way. Which one of them it was. And when. Who started it. She should try as hard as she can.

Because I don't want to have to be the one who is scared all the time now. Or to think I'm bad. I want to go to the country when she goes with that special school. I want to see the cows and the goats. And climb the trees and play on the swings. I want to show all those other little girls how well she can balance, walking on the fences for miles.

Please, remember, I scream at her. I didn't do it. You know that. It's not fair. I don't want to be trapped. No, please. I don't. Forever in the dark.

Go away, she replies. Some day I won't remember you at all.

She's grown so old now. That's what I don't like. I never expected this. Not ever. Not from someone who used to say that she would never stop climbing trees. No matter what happened. Or how many bad things she had to do. That was one thing she would never stop: She would always climb trees. Instead, she's given up just about everything. She hardly ever moves quickly. She just sits around thinking. Thinking and thinking. I can hardly believe it. That this is what adults are like.

I haven't been around too many places since the bad things finally stopped happening. The dark seemed a comfort. Though I don't know what happens there. Sometimes I think I play. With blocks or with crayons. Even with the old pictures she used to make, the ones from the circus. Sometimes I think I dream, beautiful coloured dreams. But I don't really know. Sometimes I don't remember myself at all.

There are some periods of brightness. When the light filters in with visions of places I can balance. As precious as the porcelain dolls we could never afford in the windows of stores. As soft or as fierce as the stuffed animals in F.A.O. Schwarz. The ones we would make stories about, times we could laugh and rest. The only problem is she never talks to me about those places, not the way she once did.

She does call me sometimes. Though I don't think she does that on purpose, not anymore. She's too much like Wendy in Peter Pan. So grown up and dignified. She refuses to remember where the border crossings are located, even if it's not "on until morning," and never has been. For us, on until morning was just a way to get through the bad things.

So even when she wants me to play with her, she doesn't know how to ask. She hardly remembers our special language at all. She must do something without thinking to make things change. It's like waking up after the gas, all bright colours, and suddenly I find myself there talking to her. Telling her things. What I think, or what she should do. I don't know how she understands me, but those times she seems to. She wails too, calling out to me, but even then, I don't think she hears herself.

I always come. Just the way I always did. Because it usually happens when she remembers the bad things. That's happening more and more with the new doctor she's going to. This one doesn't make her play with blocks. With him she just sits and talks: What adults do. They make up stories with pictures in their minds as bright as books. That's the only fun part of getting to know them. Their bodies are useless.

The only thing she does with any grace at all is ski. It's sort of like tree-climbing, except she can't swing by her arms anymore. The mountains where she goes are beautiful, and the movement almost as pretty as the trapeze artists. Only she hardly does that at all. She calls it being responsible. She has work to do, she says, talking to herself. A family of her own to take care of. I just call it being tired.

The blocks were much more fun than this droning on and on. I told her how much I hate the new doctor but she doesn't seem to care. I know she heard me. I just know it. It was a very short statement. Very clear. I hate that man, I said. And she flinched. So I know she's just pretending she didn't. She's just the same as always that way. Though she doesn't stick her fingers in her ears.

But she's gotten used to this. Process, she calls it. This process. It must be what they taught her at that special school. To enjoy building block towers with her words. And then looking at them from all sides. Before knocking them down. Without moving a muscle, except in her mouth. They both seem to enjoy that.

The difference is that he knows what he's doing. He's better at this than the rest of them. He knows just what to ask, while she doesn't even think she's saying anything. Maybe she's grown stupid as well as clumsy. Or maybe she doesn't remember. How dangerous talking can be. She would be ashamed if it all came out.

I remember. I remember very well. How hard she worked at keeping it all inside. It's just harder for me to remind her now. To give her a clear picture of what that was like. The way it's difficult for her to recognize me.

So I just listen to them talk. To the way they go on and on. It's boring. Even if I'm starting to pick up a lot of new words. And to talk the way she does. At least a little. Maybe that means I'm starting to grow up. I'm not sure I want that.

There is one thing I've noticed that's better than all the things I could do before. More powerful even than the visions I used to send her. Something amazing. Though I didn't invent it. She did. So it's her fault. Her problem. Not mine.

I don't even think she knows she did it. What it meant to tell me to go away. Go away you dirty pro-mis-cu-ous circus person, she said. And that put me in charge of the memories. They're mine now. And she's never even guessed what it means.

Listen closely, it's a secret. It means: I can tell her anything. Anything I want.

She'll have to believe what I say. She won't know how not to. Or when. Her body still remembers something that makes her want to tear at it. To take razor blades or knives, the little ones with the sharpest blades, and cut herself up, or at least leave marks. She still wants signs along her arms and legs of the shame she can't help feeling. Even if she can't remember where it comes from. Anymore than she can remember carving those same signs into her dolls. But it lets her know something happened. Something she should maybe leave alone.

Right there at the edge of memory, beyond the small tiny bad things she can recall when she tries. That kiss inside her mouth. That time with the cigarette butt. The hands on her body that just didn't quite seem right, or the way she sat naked on the chair.

And I can tell her more. Things that will seem right. Things her body can feel. Things she made me do. I can make an image of looking directly at that place between a man's legs. Before I had to put her mouth there. And then the smell will come back. Not just of that thing but of the room, the pantry with its old wood and its old copper sink. That dripped until the sink turned green, the smell of copper always in the room. She will remember that, and her nostrils will flare, and it will all become real. All of it except me.

But she will know that it's true. Just as she won't know where she is for a moment. Her head will feel light the way it did when they gave her those drugs, and she will shake her head and shake it, but the image won't go away. Not until she says, Oh God there's more, I didn't know there was more. And then after that I can tell her whatever I want.

That she was so-do-mized or forced to admin-is-ter oral sex. She loves those big words now. They use them a lot in that doctor's office. Big words that you can balance on, like the edge of a razor blade, that stop you from feeling the cut of what really happened. I can watch her trying to do that. String the wire between the blocks in her mind. She makes her voice very flat. Very smooth. It doesn't go up and down the way mine does. But she always falls off anyway. Because she loses track. The way she did when she fell off the fence. Then she starts to whimper. And rock back and forth.

I never did that. It didn't matter how bad it got. Even when I walked along the picture frames as I felt that man's hands, her mother's boyfriend, the one who kicked her mother's head in, reaching up under her nightgown and playing with her. Maybe even attempting to rape her. I could say that too.

That's not a big word, it's a little one. I didn't have to learn that word from the doctor. It doesn't protect you from anything. I learned it from her brother's friend. A long time ago. Not that he ever did it, he just talked about it a lot. And looked at me. Maybe I'll tell her that too. Or that her mother was sleeping next to that man. Too drunk to know.

She really hated him. Sometimes lying in her bed at night, she can smell him. Only she doesn't know where it comes from. The smell or the hate. If it's what he did to her in the kitchen or on the bed or just the fact that one day he took her for a haircut in her blue jeans and they cut her hair, in a crewcut just like a boy's. She remembers that clearly. It was another mark of shame. Something that set her apart. That and her torn pants. It made her different from the other pretty little girls.

Maybe she did want to be a boy, too. Maybe that's part of the shame. And fighting so much. Maybe she wanted to grow one of those things between her legs that got to be boss of the bad things. That made you feel big instead of cut up. At least that's what she thought.

Sometimes she would pretend to be a boy when she tormented her dolls. Or with her brother and his friend. She would be a boy like them and it was just me who was the girl who got to do bad things. Dirty, dirty, dirty. Shame, shame, shame, she would say then. Because it was all my fault.

But she knew she was shameful, too. Wanting what she could never have. She fought really hard then. Beating people up. She was good at that. Then she would tell me about lace dresses. And she would dress me in them, in our minds.

She still does that sometimes when she has sex. Both the lace dresses and the pretending she's a boy. She doesn't think about what it means. Only that it's fun. A fantasy she says. She only pretends she's herself when she makes love. There's a difference. I've learned that recently.

I could tell her about her uncle, if I wanted. The one with the smile like the wolf in Little Red Riding Hood. Or about all the roomers who lived upstairs from time to time, and all the others who drank downstairs again and again. Like walking through a field of grabbing hands. There's all of them and so many of them, that even I get confused. I can't always tell the difference between what's real and what she made me imagine, there under the bed.

I think I might even hint that her father was just as bad as the rest. It won't matter that I never knew him. For all I know that's why. Maybe he's the one who started it all. It's really hard to tell. That's the part I could never get hold of either. But if I do that, it should throw her badly. He could be a skull with rotting hands, screaming, No. Don't look. Not at me. No. I don't want you to remember. Maybe that would make her stop.

I shouldn't have to tell her what a bad idea all this looking is. She should already know. If not from before, then from right now. She knows what happens when she goes to see her friends, the ones who are so much like the nice girls she wanted to meet at that school. She sometimes shows them her journal. That's what she calls it now, instead of a diary. I liked the diary better, it was bound in blue leather and had a little gold key.

Not that the lock made her feel safe. Even years after she stopped talking to me, she would still only write about the bad things in our special code. The one she can't decipher anymore. And then she would pretend they hadn't happened at all. Dear Diary and that special pen she saved for talking about the boys she had met, with their sweaty palms, in junior high.

Only now she's trying to write it all out, trying to get all the details into this plain old notebook that she carries everywhere. The pages are already stained and dog-eared as she opens it again and again trying to find the textures of the things she doesn't know. She works at it painstakingly. Day after day. Pressing her pen hard into the page. The way she did when she covered me up with black crayon. She doesn't seem to know bad things aren't hidden there. Under the surface of the page.

She always shows it to one of those friends when she's done. Look what I've discovered, she says, pointing to the blue scribbled words. Look at how I'm putting this together. And she talks about how she plans to type it up, maybe she'll even publish it, maybe that will help make it all real.

Her friend remains silent for a minute. This is what always happens. Then she shakes her head. This is very private, she says. Very difficult. Only it sounds like Shsh. The way I always remember her saying, Shsh. A pained expression on her face.

But her friend smiles then. It's a quiet smile. Sweet. Pitying. Not like the new doctor, but like the old one with the blocks. Who always looked at her and said, That's good, dear. You're obviously very bright. Then told her to be different. The way her mother's friends did. Or her aunt.

If you keep doing these things, saying these things, you'll worry your mother, they would say. She has enough to worry about, don't you think. She's not very well, you know. That's what they called the drinking. And you have enough things to do. Good things. Wonderful things. You can be a good little girl. I know you can. You don't have to do bad things to get attention. And she would shiver. Even if they didn't mean the same kind of bad things.

That's what her friend does. First she says, This is wonderful. You're obviously onto something here. Then she tells her she has to be careful. This friend understands. But her other friends might not. They might be worried. Or worse. She might give them cause to worry about her. And it's almost like the friend is pointing.

After that the friend calls that writing dangerous. Dangerous material. You should stop forcing yourself to look at it, she says. Maybe you're not ready, you don't know what might happen as a result. It's too potent. Maybe you'll just find it all too much. And I do want you to stay with us, you know.

And then the friend pats her hand. I don't want you to, well, you know, to break down.

Or sometimes she talks differently. Or maybe that's another one. Who says, There's a lot of this stuff around. Everyone's doing it. She means writing about bad things. You're so original. Do original work. You should take on something else. You'd think women were nothing but victims. It might make it hard for people to take your other work seriously, for them to hear the other important things you have to say.

I think the only good place to be when bad things happen is far away. I think that's what they're saying. It's certainly what I learned. That's why I liked the picture frames so much. And the mouldings. They were always good places to be. Up so very high.

So maybe bad things are good as long as they stay on the page. Someone else's page. Where they can never come too close. Or make you dirty, too. When you read about faraway bad things it's en-light-en-ing. If you listen carefully, you get to understand. And feel sorry. When you do bad things, it's hard to believe there isn't something wrong with you. No one has to listen to you then. They just feel sorry.

I think that's the way it goes. Maybe I haven't grown up enough to understand the trick yet. Like I don't know where the rabbits come from that the magician pulls from the hats.

At least they don't treat the faraway bad things they read about the way her brother's friend did those magazines with pictures of bad things he always brought over. He rubbed them with his fingers. And let his face get red. They just roll that word around in their mouths as they turn the pages. Even her pages. They love that word.

This is very en-light-en-ing, BUT, they say. The longest word is the but.

It's when she hears that but that she starts to hear what she used to tell me. It's like the word gets longer and longer until she hears, You ought to be ashamed. You ought to be ashamed. Over and over. And she doesn't hear en-light-en-ing either. She hears pro-mis-cu-ous.

It's funny what happens then. Since she can't put her fingers in her ears, grown-ups don't do that, she kind of goes away from them. And her whole world turns grey. Except for the blue words on the white page. So it's not like me going into the light, but like her coming into the dark with me.

I'm sure that if she knew I was here she would get even by shouting. And chanting her little chants. Go to Hell if you tell, things like that. She would probably call me a dirty pro-mis-cu-ous circus person again, and say I wrote all those words there when she wasn't looking, even if I don't know how to write that language. I'm only just learning to speak it well. To sound grown up.

Only she thinks she's all alone and she has to take it all on herself, just the way she did when I first met her. When she felt so ashamed. When she was so sure it was her own fault. That's the way she is now. Trying to call that doctor and looking at all the knives she has in her kitchen and lining up the pills in her medicine cabinet. Before she goes into her closet and tears the clothes off the rack, and retreats to the very back, and pulls them on top of her, and sits in there, her head pillowed on her arms, and beats her head against the wall while she cries and cries.

I spend that time with her. The way I did when I first came from the circus. I know I could laugh at her if I wanted to. See what you've done, I could say. See how stupid you are. See what those nice girls really think of you. You were right all along.

But I don't. Because it's then she's willing to listen to me. Or at least to try. Though mostly she just hears a vague babbling no matter how hard she tries. That's why I usually just cry with her and send her images. I don't try for memories then. I do pretty pictures full of light. The kind she finds in her dreams. The kind I find in mine. That have made me like her so much, the times I've gotten to see her, even with everything else she's done, all these years. The kind that remind me of the things we shared. The fence and the dolls and the pictures of the circus and the tightrope. The way I still love it when she skis. That's why I send her visions of the mountains.

Beautiful in blue and white, mostly blue and white, the long views from way up at the top. But in green, too, green and brown, and full of air and silence: The spaces that I love. I think that will take her mind off her shame, off all her difficulties. Just like it did when I asked her to watch me climbing along the edges of the mouldings. Or the way her friends tell her to get into something different, to take her mind off her problems.

It doesn't work very well. Not that she isn't comforted. Not that she doesn't finally fall asleep exhausted watching the mountains far below. It's that she won't stop.

She won't even believe me about that doctor. She thinks

she's found a noble cause. Made more noble by her friends'
dislike. She thinks their disapproval will purify her. Like a
trial by fire. If she can just bear it long enough to find out.

She carries those words around with her. To Find Out.
Like a standard a knight could carry. Curiosity is her motto.
The way they taught her at that school.

She thinks her life is one of their puzzles, the kind she
always loved to solve, the kind that brought her so much
praise. She thinks it's just a matter of getting all the pieces in
the right order. That everyone will praise her when she does.
Even her friends will praise her. And recognize what she's
done. Returning healed from her quest. They won't believe
she's dirty and shameful anymore. She won't believe it herself.

Maybe I could have agreed with her once. Maybe I even
wanted her to do that. The problem is I don't think she'll find
out anything I don't already know. I just think she'll find me.
And if you ask me, that's what this process is all about.
Finding me. Blaming me. Doing it all again.

Not just letting me out, pushing me out. Letting that
doctor insert a long fishing line down her throat. To pull
me out wriggling so they can look at me all over. And I don't
want anyone to do that anymore. Look at me like that.
I prefer the dark to being poked and prodded the way her
brother's friends did, or that man, or all the others.

The way her mother did to her that time she got the
ringworm. Or those people who thought they were helping.
When she had to get her mother, drunk and singing. Off the
subway. Making me stand there. With a smile on my face.

Besides. I'm probably ugly now. She's probably right
about that. You can't do the things I've done, live the way I've
lived, and not be ugly. Maybe I'm all covered in sores the way
she was, only worse, because maybe they're cut and bleeding.
Maybe I look the way she made me imagine her that time
under the bed. Maybe my face is all contorted, and my body,
too, the springs twisting in and out. Or maybe it's all rotted

away just like those images I used to send her. Just a stiff rotted twig, or skinny like an insect. Maybe I'd be able to do even less with it than she can.

I might not be able to balance on the furniture the way I used to, or in the doctor's hair, to make her laugh. If she laughed now, it would be to make me feel bad. I know that. Maybe she would even crush me like I really was a bug, before I could say anything. Just to hear my body pop, the way her brother and his friends liked to do with the big black beetles that got into the house.

I can't let her do that, can't you see?

That's why I've decided I'll finally teach her a lesson. It's my turn now. I know I have the power. I've never even been able to shut her in the dark, but there's something I can do. I know that now. And I'm better than she is. I won't just do it for me. I'll make us both safe. That's what she really wants anyway. It's what she's always wanted. Not adventure. Not beautiful circus tricks: Safety.

Sometimes that doctor takes her places when she goes to see him. Places inside her head. Visualizations he calls them. Guided visualizations. He's the guide. He takes her in and out of her old house. Things like that. But he's never taken her where she really wants to go. That's what I'll do.

He's asked her to try to recover the child she was. To go back to that. To enter that place, and to get her. He thinks it will make her whole. If she walks along a path and through a forest and out into an open space, where she can find herself playing. Only she never imagines it terrible the way it was, full of cold and shame and that awful sense of rotting. It's always that place in the country she went with that school, with its swings and its fences.

She sees herself as an up-set child, a vic-tim-ized child, a sorry child, a vi-olated child. She brings out all the big words for this one, going through them again and again, like those prayers her aunt used to say with those beads she carried.

Because only one thing is important. And she's got to get it right.

She's got to make sure that child is dirty only on the outside. That the child she sees will be a child anyone would want to have, one you would just have to clean up a bit, to make her ready for the nicest girl to play with. The kind of child she convinced those little girls at that special school she really was: A lovely un-der-pri-vi-leged child. She chanted that, once she heard the word. I'm un-der-pri-vi-leged, I'm not pro-mis-cu-ous, she used to say.

Such a bright and curious child would know it wasn't her fault if bad things happened to her. She would sigh a lot. And wait to be rescued. By nice people. Like the friends she has now. Or the person she likes to think she is.

That child wouldn't torment her body or her dolls. Not that child she built so long ago for the doctor with the blocks, the one she keeps building again and again with the blocks in her mind, even for this doctor now. The one she wants to see all crying and lonely inside that enclosure. Waiting for her. As if that prissy child hadn't had a companion all these years. Who knows better.

One time she's going to try to find that child. Maybe when she's alone, driving along a mountain road, or in city traffic, or walking in the park. Or maybe she'll just be sitting in her favourite attic room, doing what she does so much now, just thinking and thinking. When suddenly without hardly noticing it, she will start down that path again. Only when she sees the enclosure it's not that child she constructed like an erector set, it's not the one who pretended she never knew me, no: I'm the one who's going to be there. Me, the dirty pro-mis-cu-ous circus person, the one she let do all the bad things. I'm the one who will be playing there.

And I won't be crying. I'll be singing. And as she comes closer she'll be happy to see me. Because I won't be ugly. For the last time it will be my world and I will still be the tightrope walker and I will take a wide bow, my arms held out beside me, and I will hop up with my umbrella onto the very top of the fence that encloses me, something that erector set child would never be able to do, and I will balance there and I will walk. And the sun will glint off the spangles in my costume and it will shine all the colours of the rainbow and before she can even think to stop or call that other doctor she will climb up, too, and she will follow me with her clumsy adult body. And I will finally lead her along the fence the way I wanted to do so long ago.

Only it won't be the fence at that country place anymore. It will soon be a fence, and then a tightrope, not in the circus but in the mountains. Stretched from peak to peak so that we will be surrounded by sunlight. While below us there will stretch the forest and the river that leads far far away to the ocean. And her gaze will follow it, until it disappears into the mountains along the horizon. Her eyes fixed along the distant peaks as she will keep walking and walking, one foot in front of the other. Until there will come a moment just as we reach the top of the peak where the high wire ends on a small metal platform, a moment when I will turn and face her.

And maybe in that moment she will remember me, and maybe she will remember it all, and maybe then we will both know the whole story. But it won't matter whether she does or not because she will never write it in her journal. We will keep our little secret no matter what it is, because in that moment she will look down. And she will suddenly be afraid, and she will start to whimper, and she will remember that she is an adult, suddenly caught like a child in a world she doesn't understand, whose balance is not what it once was. And maybe she will even feel the front of her mouth, all that bridge work where her tooth was knocked out. And she will start to rock back and forth, and pretty soon she will fall.

But I'm not cruel, I told you that.

No matter how many bad things I've done or she's made

me do, I would never let her fall alone. I will not laugh at her, or chant, clum-sy grown-up, clum-sy grown-up. I will jump forward from the place where I stand, perfectly balanced, my umbrella held high, and I will grab hold of her. And hugging each other tight we will fall, fall and fall, toward that river where it glints. The two of us, turning around and around, so very slowly, like little cartoon characters under my umbrella. And it will be that time before when we were happy, falling and floating, spinning and laughing, like the dust motes in her father's study when she first drew my picture. Suspended together. Forever in the sunlight.

Hello, I will say, Don't you remember me?

PARENTHESES

( )

The world, your five-year-old son will inform you, is a story someone is telling. Maybe, it is a story I am telling, he will go on, then dissolve into giggles the way he once did with the hand that covered his mouth, as he repeats it. The world is a story I am telling. A story I am telling, a story I am telling.

You will look at him, not in horror this time, but in recognition. You will giggle, too. You think: Perhaps, it is true.

You will note how much he has grown. How you can barely lift him now, certainly not quickly or suddenly the way once you did, certainly not whirling put him down, the way that gesture entered your story. You will remember, then, how long it took before those stories of yours had a centre, how long it took to feel a teller at the centre of the tale.

To find an 'I' that could tell your world.

Those days you could barely breathe, and neither you

nor your story seemed to have a place to go. When characters would enter your mind, speak to you and march off stage. While you, ever the author of fiction, tried to contain them, give them a shape, a place to begin and end.

You did succeed sometimes. The stories taking on the shapes they needed, the shapes to move and hold the voice that spoke you, that was you — at least a part of you. Though as often as not they would shatter, multiply, reshape themselves into other voices and other moments, other pieces of yourself, often to remain only in fragments, small beginnings or endings, tiny pieces of muddled middles, the voices in your mind taking on their tone on the page, but refusing to move beyond that tone into story. Or you would refuse to push them. The way you will do sometimes with memory. Look briefly and say, Oh, yes, that, that. Refusing to enter that place.

Sometimes you would wish to prevent the alternative. The story spinning out of control to consume you, or minimally to create reams of notes that might one day be stories or books, consigned for now to the back of your filing cabinet. While others will follow out myths and legends and fairy tales, you and your brother as Hansel and Gretel, you as the child Baldur, the perfect innocent golden child, or as the hero twins of Maya myth, of *The Popul Vuh* — the book your dad gave you for your twelfth birthday. The story of Hunapuh and Xbalanque, one that will tug at you until you start to think it out in an adult voice — work still a long way into the future as your son repeats himself. The world is a story I am telling, a story I am telling.

Often you will wish to leave this process altogether. The spinning of beginnings and middles and endings, endings and beginnings and middles, story fragments dividing you and multiplying you, until you will wonder if the world is a story you are refusing to tell. Only you cannot find the location of that refusal, where it is in all these stories, if it is in these stories at all.

In therapy you will consent to a disastrous exercise. You will walk yourself into your mother's house to find out what happened there. Entering through the backyard, you will ascend the two concrete steps to the back door, open it, go past the grey stone sink and white metal-topped table to the chair on which your mother's lover, Paul Garcia, had tongue kissed you, leaving you for years with more ease with intercourse, with the clean distant, hopefully quick, fact of penetration, than with the long sensual beauty of a deep kiss. Then passing there, a place you have always acknowledged, then tried to forget, thinking instead of how he taught you to mambo with your feet on his, you will open the basement door. To find yourself looking through the rungs of the stairs, as the smell assaults you, mildew and oil, and something else, that will not allow you to walk down to the place of the tangled sheets, or to the back room behind the furnace where your brother and his friend too, poked and prodded. So that no matter how vivid the exact wrinkles on those sheets, the stripes on the mattress, you will not go down.

Instead, gathering all your strength, you paste what you hope is a pleasant smile onto your face, and rather than saying that you are overwhelmed, you open your eyes, take a deep breath and report, trying to look contained, mature, that it just isn't working. Oh, dear, you say, I don't seem to be getting anywhere with this. What you always do when something like this happens: Pretend your way through, while trying to stay as still as possible. The way you talk about never taking a step when you are unsure where the ground is. When your life is like a shape-shifting science fiction novel. Life on the holo-deck. Only you don't know who operates the controls.

Because that day when you get home you will discover that you did not leave. You are still in that house. Even if you do not quite know where.

Now, there will be no stories at all. Just the sense of entrapment washing over you, and a world grey on grey. Erasing all colour from that place in your mind we all go, where we all visualize or remember. Memory, as in your adolescence, will be a cold, New York winter fog. And this will be the first parenthesis — the first thing you think of as a parenthesis — as if you have been placed between brackets. Caught inside an informational aside whose information you cannot decipher.

At first you think all you will have to do is get out of the house. That will bring the colours back. At least that. Maybe more. Give you a world to tell. This has been an accident only. Your narrative will resume its course. You forget how you felt before this happened.

Now, you attempt to retrace your footsteps. Try different routes. Going out first to the front door, and trying that. Then up to the first floor and through the first floor window and onto the stoop next door. Then up to your room, whichever of your rooms, but always the top floor like the attic room you are actually in, going up the ladder to the roof and onto the roof next door, and down the fire escape of the secretarial school, as you did many times. Or, most dramatic of all, what you never tried but thought you could if worse came to worst, out your window, and onto the drainpipe next door, then over onto the fire escape as before, and out into the yard, and across the fences to the street. While as you write it down, this last escape route, you will notice how you write windpipe, windpipe instead of drainpipe, window and drainpipe intermixing as your mind races ahead to the next thought.

You will take your hand off the keyboard, and reach for your throat, the way you often do, in so many situations. The windpipe has always been your escape route.

You will think of Scheherazade then, that other one saved by her windpipe, sinking your mind into the structure of the episodic novel. Things you can think about. Not story, but the nature of story. How it works, how it functions, as your own story mind remains blank, full of the dull grey feature-less aching, the life without even the briefest shadow of pleasure, or the rainbow of a sharper pain, that when you cannot think of some intellectual puzzle, will bring you to your knees.

You think of how, at least in European literature, the episodic novel is the first form of the novel, with its move from the book of morality tales, to the teller at the centre of the tale. Someone who tells the episodes, usually of the encounters of others, while doing something, arranging something, fleeing something, encountering something. Like the *Women's Decameron* — whose real title is other, but which you found in the library titled that way, not the modern Russian one, self-consciously titled by its author, but a book by a female contemporary of Cervantes — the teller a woman at a party, like you at so many receptions following papers or performances, going from group to group, telling tales. Though you do not remember why she tells, any more than you can understand why you do — unless it is to avoid something else. The deeper story which will manifest only as chaos.

You think of how Scheherazade told to avoid death. Each story a postponement of final closure, this the greatest truth of narrative: If you are telling, you are still alive. Even torturers know this — you have certainly translated enough testimonies — and take advantage. Held in isolation, the need for narrative is, as often as not, what makes prisoners speak. Though perhaps what is told will not be the truth, but just something meant to please. While the truth would explode the world into chaos. The way Scheherazade had to be calm, had to be charming, had to be indirect, since, likely as not, letting the secret out, the secret of her own imminent demise, trying to persuade directly, or sinking into grief, whining or howling, no, no, no, would have killed her.

You come up with a wonderful conceit then. Letting your mind wander further into the arena of the intellect, surpressing its emotions, except in the small giggle that explodes from your mouth as it comes to you in the restaurant. A thank-god-we've-escaped kind of restaurant. Perhaps, a thank-god-we-were-never-there. With its decor for touring poverty and damage. Its spaces wide, accommodating. Its wine bold — tasteful as well as tasty. The sun shining in just enough for you never to hear the squeaking of rats or mice behind the slats, or feel the heat of the fire — the building did burn not too long ago, leaving the scars but not the smell — knowing you cannot get out the door. Or even to fall, as you once did, face down on the floor tiles, too hurt to move, to watch them pattern out in their ordered circles of seven, like multiplying stories.

The floor tiles at the entrance have shocked you, moving you back into the grey space, suddenly just like them. White ceramic turned to grey. Deeper grey almost black, the grouting between. You know you have a story there, that there is a story there, even as you encounter chaos, and the desire to play with your food. Always play with your food.

You lift your fork as you say, looking out to the patio, What if Scheherazade were an incest survivor? What if the Sultan never intended to kill her at all? What if she never told the tales, not then, not out loud, but merely told them to herself as she let him do what he wished with her?

Your smile will be broad then, despite the hollow inside, knowing you have created a trajectory. You have their attention. You must go on. But you like the formulation. Springing as it has, whole, into your mind. You know you can elaborate it. Mostly, or simply, because it makes sense to you. And it assuages the ache the floor tiles cause. This rising to objectivity, to a strange kind of fun.

You see, you might continue, it would have been fairly typical. That she was trained at home. That happens all the time in what is now called the incest family, perhaps even consciously in this case. Her family trying to protect her from death, not through keeping her innocent, but by giving her knowledge. Erotic knowledge. It wasn't story-telling her family trained her in, though some might say the erotic, too, is a narrative. Father or brother or uncle, would have taught her exactly what to do, to give pleasure to a man. While what the mother did, helpless to stop any other part of the family dynamic, was teach her to tell stories to herself, to keep her mind away from what was done to her. A classic dissociation. So it wasn't that she would be purer, just better, than all the rest.

   You must see it that way, you could go on, this dissociated world a story you are telling. It is in the nature of the story, your hands expanding, in that perfect patriarchal family they always speak of in the incest literature. With the family's isolation and absolute paternal rule, where the mother is complicit. She might even train the dutiful daughter — you are back to that — pushing her into the hands of the Sultan. Not with a repertoire of stories, but with a whole series of erotic inventions, the thousand and one ways to manipulate men given to the incested daughter you have already thought about. So that when father was through, or uncle or brother, or old family friends, or just when daughter was ready, she could go from one captivity to another.

And the sultan, of course, would be completely besotted with her.

You will suppress a laugh as you imagine Scheherazade telling stories to herself just to think herself elsewhere, outside the room in which she waits. Which you see, somehow, like the floor tiles, complex but repetitive, grey on grey with rich pearl and mother-of-pearl and gold brocade, a perfect place into which to invite the Sultan, where she would eat with him the most precious sweetmeats, in preparation for their erotic acts. The stories in her mind getting her ready for them. And for him. So that she would never fully be there. While it would just be from that texture and that waiting that her stories would grow, stories she never told the Sultan, marvellous inventions, of faraway places and adventures, woven by one who had never been outside the women's quarters — of her own house or of the palace — as she would watch each story change and mutate and reproduce, the way yours have done. Only hers would never stop

You think of how each night behind the grey on white brocade curtains of her bed, she would do exactly as the Sultan asked, developing an amazing subtlety of erotic repertoire. At the same time as she would seem, well, just not completely, you know, there. While that need of hers to absorb herself into herself would produce his need of her in an erotic obsession both realized and unrealized, the kind men so often speak about, or pornography does. No one, absolutely no one, they say in longing, could do the things she could.

Only they do. Of course they do, you find yourself thinking. Do and could and did and all the time. In beds and back seats and brothels and alleyways and open meadows and airplane bathrooms and taxis. On chairs and tables and kitchen counters and tree branches and oak desks and floors and car hoods. Among sheets and leaves and dust and detritus and flower petals. So that it was that quality of withdrawal, you conclude, of being both captured and absent that led to the obsession, being both pliant and rigid, close and distant, in need and never needing anything, until the what of what she did that no one else could do was really expressed in the fact that no matter what she did she did not quite do it.

While he, who possessed her every night, would increasingly feel that he never did quite do it either, that he never really had, that he never really had had her, but that he, too, like her, like you, was always waiting. And that what she made him wait for, even if he didn't know what it was, was better than anything he had ever had with anyone. With that pure grey-white distance still there, a distance so pure it became purity itself, the perfect still unstoried moment.

Until he wouldn't or couldn't ever order her death, nor expect her betrayal. As she traced her stories on his skin, her self elsewhere. After all, how could he be betrayed by a force of nature, as alien to him as a tree. The way that figure always is, the sensual child-woman, or even women in general, often enough when you encounter them in literature. Without it mattering that they have not been produced by nature at all, but as often as not, result from the wiles of oppression. While he, if he were more worldly wise, more cynical, a Garcia Marquez character perhaps, he might just shrug and tell you she would be unable to betray him, who she had never truly been with. The way it is in *El Amor y Otros Demonios*.

Until the day would come that she would become sick in the mornings, and no matter how far away she had gotten to be, no matter how ethereal, no matter how scattered and multiplied and not fully there, she would be suddenly centred in that body which had meant so little to her, centred in its vomitings and its sweatings and its peeings and its shittings, something that she had not been in so long she would barely know what that body was, that was congratulated at every turn on becoming truly a woman: A mother.

And she might hate it and pound at her belly, or love it

and rub that same place in triumphant pride, all her labour of disappearance at last rewarded with so specific a becoming, but either way she would eventually bear the Sultan a son and he would marry her, and declare the son his heir, and she would be the Queen Mother, ruler of the women's quarters. While out of love of her, of appreciation for all that time she had given him, and for her motherhood, for how, now, she would look upon her baby son, counting his fingers and his toes, putting his small mouth to her breast, looking from his head to the window, never quite there and always there for the baby too, after that the Sultan would restrain himself from his nightly demands. Though, of course, sometimes, he would go to hear her stories, the ones perfected in her mind during their erotic games.

While she, of course, growing older, embarrassed at her youthful dependence, on his hands his mouth that thing between his legs, the need to please or to be sheltered, or just for her life, the need to have at least that, that had caused her always to use her body as she had been taught to use it — why exactly will never quite be made clear — would tell the story as it has come down to us, speaking with the authority of the fruitful grandmother granted limited authority under patriarchy.

I kept him at bay until the wedding, she would say. I kept him at bay. The others are all dead. I was the only one. But I did it: I kept him at bay.

She would tell, then, how she told in order to preserve her purity, not just from death, but from the fate worse than death that was its sullying. She would never ever speak of the way it was. But tell them that it was only through the love of her mother, the wise council of her father or her brother, as to what she had to do to please the Sultan — with her purity and her stories, keeping him forever there with her in her infinite postponement of climax, the climax of narrative —

that she had triumphed, and come to occupy her present position in the world. With no more need to tell how once she had needed and used her body — to stay alive, to manipulate and control, to comfort and to be comforted, only marginally inside the physical world, here and not here, there and not there, while her mind would wander down the corridors of narrative. And of time.

And then she would spread her hands out on her lap, covered in its delicate grey and gold brocades, and begin to tell once more. Beautiful inventions. Story after story.

You will spread your own hands on the cloth napkin in your lap, pleased with your invention. Pleased, even, with its reception: The hearty laughter of those you sit with. You will shiver only when you ask yourself: But what if she had borne the sultan a daughter, not a son? What then? No Queen Mother, just a daughter-producing drone. What would she have done with that mirror of herself? What trained her in?

In any case, your invention, floating there, elegant, lovely, will not help you find your own way back to story, your own story. Not even to a book of examples — morality tales without a teller at their centre — the form that preceded the episodic novel. Not anymore. There is no longer even that. Much less a teller to order them. No, it seems there is nothing for you there. Just intellectual conceits and false laughter. And the multiplying floor tiles. Grey, threatening.

You remember those along so many hallways in New York. The ones in the doorway of your mother's house. At so many thresholds. You feel nauseous. Retreat into a kind of shock. While your hands still move, you see your own laughter. You. Miles away.

You will try to move along the floor tiles. Follow them. Find out where they are. Perhaps in your mother's house. Perhaps right at the door. You convince yourself you are right there. Instead, find yourself falling. The octagonal tiles seeming to form a pattern which catches you. Still in grey. While you clutch your throat. Still watch. The voices only babbling now. Without direction or purpose. Seeming to take you nowhere. And it will be your partner, Tom, not you, who will tell your therapist what has happened. So that you will be greeted with the words: But have you ever really left?

It will be the first time you realize that it's true. The therapist did not leave you trapped there, when you broke off that exercise in the middle. Nor was it really a return. There has always been some part of you stuck in that house. You think it is as if you have started switching places, and you do not always know where the part of you that got out, that got away, the one with the spark, the charisma, the brilliance, the you you think you have always been, you no longer know where she is. Who she is. And what you are, whatever you it is that laughs and smiles and goes through the motions is just an overview. Hollowed out. An intellectual construct. You know, your hand on your throat, your throat becoming numb, dysfunctional now, it is imperative that you get her, that you get yourself, out of that house. All of you this time.

Because you will have noticed and noted down, how the grey imbues your days. How all the colours are in the past, trapped with her. And you will not be able to survive long without them.

You will watch your son, up in your attic room with you, still laughing and repeating: The world is a story I am telling, a story I am telling, and — thinking of Scheherazade again — something will occur to you.

That the teller at the centre of that tale escaped from that centre, that unsafe centre, into fictional margins, fictional episodes. You wonder if, if you can create a safe fictional centre, perhaps the episodes, the varied and real episodes, the ones that tell you who you are, perhaps they will become clear.

This is, perhaps, when you name her. Decide to call her Jane Dark. Treat her as if she were separate. As if you can sing to her, read to her, ask her questions, make jokes. Comfort that hurt child who has had to stay behind.

You decide to leave the exercise given in therapy, for another, an earlier one. Only you will make it different. The safe place you will imagine will not be a place in the country as you imagined escaping in your childhood, as you escape now into the Rocky Mountains, but a room. You will build a safe room, into which she can come. Alter the form of your mother's house, and her control in it.

Like your room, the one in your mother's house, your attic room now, it will be at the top of the house. Only it will be the only room and its door will be secure. You will spend time on this. In near sleep, and in waking moments. Think that, if you can do this, then you will entice her into movement. Minimally, into looking around. Even as you try to write her out of the house, letting a story take over your mind without ever being written, then later writing it again and again until it is too big to be accommodated and is left, as you begin the process of drawing when you cannot find colours or words in your present life, your drawings each a small light out of the dark, out of the grey, for Jane out of the dark, Jane Dark out of the dark, you, too, now, out of the dark where you have become trapped with her. Even as you try to imagine, to make for her a house that is not that house, but another one, a room that is not your room, but hers alone. But where you will always talk to her, if she wants. You do not wish to isolate her to contain her, to keep her separate from yourself. The way you once did, leaving her there.

You try to make it a turret room, where you can see out each window, in all directions. The way you once knew an artist in

New York, Diane Arbus's lover Marvin Israel, who had a two storey cupola for a studio, at the very top of an office tower, the 22nd floor on 28th Street costing him 26 dollars a month, if you've got it right, all twenties anyway, and probably worth hundreds of thousands now. Only her room won't be on top of an office building, it will be an old Victorian house that you will put in the middle of highways and old warehouses, you see it very clearly right on the corner down by the Gowanus Canal, the high overpass to accomodate the ships coming in to one side, basketball courts to the other, but no other houses around anywhere. And all of it in those days stinking of oil and garbage and loneliness, that they are trying to clean up now — your sister-in-law sends you notices — make the warehouses into lofts with boat slips, only no one can figure out how to make the concrete sea walls needed to accommodate the ocean tides accommodate the yuppies' need for a view from the boat.

You have always needed a view. The way you needed a view even then. The way she needs a view, you are sure of it. Even as you build one other house in your mind. One across the street with a bar which will symbolize all the bars of your childhood, and an easier walk, and easier to get away from, to spy on, to see what's happening, than the longer sadder walk from Montero's. And besides, it does happen that way often enough, one old house and one old tenement, shops or bars on its first floor, left in a neighbourhood that has become highways and high flyovers, grey steel against grey to pink night sky. Because in your story it will be always night, with the asphalt black of the ground and perhaps one or two stunted trees, not ginkgoes but ailanthus, the tree that grows in Brooklyn for which the book is named, you remember them, there were hundreds with their strange skunky stink — in backyards and vacant lots and coming up through concrete. While you will give Jane all of the top floor, the cupola, to see out of. The world a story to tell, but from a distance. Where no one can make her do, or even see, what she does not wish to.

You will start to draw then. Slowly. Try to make the route clear. Thinking: If I make the colours real, with real pencils, real chalks, maybe I can feel them. Maybe she can see them. They will be a game. One we can put away. The way we can our toys, or our tools. So that you place them in a book. As if they are beside the point. Each one a parenthesis. Or an episode. Or just a holding operation. Not a narrative, but a stasis. A way to stay. To remain. To endure.

You will move slowly, brightly, in brilliant colours, back to your mother's house. You will sit with her then as her hand reaches forward to help you make each bright image. While the rest will be grey. Grey Jane grey room grey life: Lady Jane Grey. Sometimes you will see her there, right beside you, or behind you, fading in that grey, that featureless dark. The creatures of the true dark are the ones who are the whitest white, white body white hair white eyes, the way you will see her contin-ue to bleach, until her transparency scares you, that one day she will not be there at all, this Jane Dark in the dark, the one you need so badly: But only emptiness. Until you redouble your efforts, move your hand more fiercely across the page, rub colour more harshly into it, as you try to feel in how her hand moves with yours that she, too, is infusing with colour. The way you hope colour will infuse your days.

It will take more than a year. Stroke by stroke. Image by image. Parenthesis by parenthesis. Until what you've drawn can become episodes, and she the teller at the centre of your tale. Tales she will move through, bright hued, no longer trapped in the dark or even in the room you have created for her. So that perhaps this thing might finally be a picaresque, the next stage in the novel, a life and times, each episode happening to a moving and multi-dimensional narrator.

And the world, a story you are telling.

(( ))

There will be other parentheses too. Into which to slip.
Intellectual asides. Emotional asides. Places to get stuck, trying to decipher their information. Sometimes, especially from
inside, you will wish to name them. The way naming things,
we always feel we gain control. You like to think of them
with titles: The Parenthesis of Sadness, The Parenthesis of
Trickery — sort of like The Sea of Despond, or marsh or
swamp, or whatever it was. Those allegorical challenges in
Pilgrim's Progress, so much less interesting than morality
tales, but linear, directional, ever upward and onward. Just
that chronological puritanism you always refuse, preferring
the digressive, those things that go around the point, refusing
to come to it, Scheherazade's postponement of closure.

Now you want it different. Clear. Concise. Over. Mostly
over. Like writing an academic paper. Coming to the point
because you just don't want to do it any longer. Wishing you
could do that here, with the titles the only things that tell you

that maybe, whatever these parentheses are, maybe they will have a point, at least a meaning.

This next one will be The Parenthesis of Rage. It makes you remember what had brought up Scheherazade, and what had made her into an incest survivor. And this time you will be inside a roaring vortex, multi-coloured, but without form. Just the one voice raging. You do not really know at what. Or how the rage became so deep. It will not be until you hear a seductive haunting voice which answers it, curved toward you like the closing parenthesis, that you will begin to under-stand. How all this comes together, rage and rape and colours and grey and the hand tracing, letters, figures, you, the world. But this: An academic conference again. Full of a roaring beneath the cool words.

In another moment, you think, it would have been just an accidental, if mean-spirited, throwaway line to let the audience know who it is that still occupies the centre of the world, who is the teller in the academic tale. Instead, for you, it will connect your survivor Scheherazade to another story. Where once more, women tell stories of the court.

You will be sitting there on the panel, calm, composed, trying to be the person you have always been. And it will be that kind of meandering conversation, the look at us aren't we important sitting here kind, where the panellists speak as if in their living room, demonstrating their own importance to the audience by acting as if the audience weren't there. So that the conversation will move from influences on each one's work, to influences on the work of others, to influences on work in the twentieth century to current issues of voice and suppression of voice and who speaks and who learns to speak. Suppression and resistance and appropriation and authentic-ity when one of the other panellists will assert that no loss of language — or speech or story — could matter, since great writers — look at the example of Vladimir Nabokov — should be able to switch languages to write.

And maybe it will be childish of you, after all you have no experience of Nabokov, not really, there was always the bloated sense of the trap of fifties America about him that made you move directly to the Latin Americans — as you moved to Latin America — of a similar time, to Cortázar and Borges and Asturias and Castellanos just to get away, but all you will be able to think of is *Lolita*. And it will hardly matter that *Lolita* was not Nabokov or even that he might have wished to deconstruct such a fantasy, but no statement will come to mind to counter such a broad and, you think, silly, assertion. To say that the language of a people is not the choice of a great writer but the basis on which any such choice is made possible, that we all reinvent language and with it identity, but that those identities, their art their language their use objects, are the most precious and perhaps the only treasure we have, the destruction of them, like the destruction of the Maya codices, a form of genocide, and of betrayal of what most basically makes us human. It does not even occur to you to continue to speak of your dad's loss of language, of his first language beaten out of him — as it was out of so many Native people — and the influence of that on your life and your writing — no, the only statement that will come into your mind — and it will silence you, is: *Lolita* was written the summer I turned eleven.

You will know immediately it is childish even to think that. More, you will feel the rage that accompanies it as a childish betrayal. Your mind, your rage, betraying you. How could you even potentially have held against a great writer all these years those men standing against the refrigerator admiring your still childish body? How could your hands tremble now, and not at this assault on the meaning of language loss, but at the images assaulting your mind? You will have to breathe deeply before you can leave those images, those men wondering if you were a nymphet, how precisely could they tell if you were a nymphet, looking at your chest and asking — even your dad — when you would get a sweater with the bumps in it. A harmless enough question, except for the other questions in those other men's eyes. The ones who see you differently — and act upon it — in the drinking nights around your mother's table.

But it will not leave you, that thought, those images, even as the conversation eddies around you. Now moving on to encompass the idea of narrative as chronology and mere chronology, when to you — even now that you have lost it — story is narrative and story is again and again and always. An again and always you would wish to recover. An again and always at the core of the self you seem to have lost. Inside these wild voices these wild vortices whose origins you cannot trace, which tear you apart instead of letting you accrete, the way you might wish to assert language and identity are accreted.

You will try again to keep track. Stay on the level of the intellectual discussion around you. Narrative as the begats of the Bible. Of patriarchal ownership and oppression. Only you cannot even go there. Join that. Think instead of the Chilam Balaam books, narratives of ownership as narratives of resistance. Even that will not tempt you. To consider, or to elaborate, even to speak. Instead you find yourself, your mind asserting the one comment you have made, that the idea of narrative as chronology is very much involved with culture, and the considered nature of time. You will make another circle. Not among begats, but inside what is considered the first novel ever written: *The Tale of Genji*.

Another parenthesis will open. A parenthesis inside The Parenthesis of Rage. This one full of information. Information you feel you can use. In that, perhaps, more like a footnote. The Footnote of Betrayal. That's right: The Footnote of Betrayal inside The Parenthesis of Rage.

For a moment you will not know if you are back in eleventh-century Japan or in your mother's kitchen. Her kitchen or her bedroom. And if what you witness in the story place in your mind is a man in a bathrobe, or Prince Genji in his most beautiful kimono. All you will know for a moment is the metal taste of an anger which cannot speak.

You will pause, your hand, once more, over your throat. The silenced witness. Waiting. Waiting. You, the part you call yourself, waiting: An inch behind your skin.

They are back on seduction. Story seduction. Not seduction stories. Whether by women or nymphets. No, this is about how story wishes to seduce you. Wants to make you tell it. Taking you away from the purity of language, of utterance, of the moment just for itself, to embrace — what — memory, history, herstory, story time, contextuality. Above all, you think, contextuality. The siren call of context. Cunt X, you think for a moment, joking to yourself. Once you heed its voice you will be spoiled, rendered impure, forever. That old argument about women, so prevalent at the turn of the twentieth century. Even the nymphet already a seductress, the snake of evil already in her. So that you would follow her anywhere, as Humbert Humbert did Lolita. And story the same: it may look innocent, but enter its grasp and you will never be the same again. Which, of course, is story's intent. As it was Eve's. To make you eat of the apple of knowledge. And of context. Make you not simply live your narrative, but examine it. What power never wishes to do. And confuses ignorance with perfection. Living in the moment with refusing consequences.

You go back to looking at the wall. The clock on it. Back to thinking. Wondering at it, what this thing is. It goes without saying you have heard it before. The impurity of story like the fall from grace, turning it over in your mind, the way you always turn things over in your mind. The way you always have turned things over in your mind, perhaps even at the bottom of the slide, certainly in those days — it is strange what you do remember clearly, when you can remember so little. You, already, your head in your hands, sitting halfway up the staircase between the third and fourth floor, between the world of your room and the world below — worrying at the nature of story by deconstructing nursery rhyme. How, after all, could those blind mice manage to chase anybody at all, and why would they want to? What did the weasel do when it went pop? And what about those flying baked black-birds? Or feeling the tragedy of bedtime stories. Why was it, after all, the little bear who always lost everything? Why was it the Gingerbread Boy who always had to die?

Perhaps, another form of protection. Applying moral and intellectual order to story instead of to the world around you. Now you want to do both. Only you cannot apply order to a world you cannot know, cannot see.

You know that this denigration of story goes back a long way, and, though hardly universal, is seen in many places. It's pos-sible, you even think, that this need to escape context might come up somewhere shortly after the institution of hierarchy, of patriarchy. When, at least in the case of the Judeo-Christian tradition, individual and collective responsibility for story making, for world making, is avoided, by giving it to one god, one teller, who tells one story, who supervises time and is above it all. Thus circumventing the essential wound of language. When to know language is to know otherness is to know death is to know we are never ourselves is to know we are only ourselves. Is to know story. The beyond oneself that is always what we make between us. Instead, throw it away. Say He did it. Him. God. Him. He did. It's not ours. We won't own it. Not our world. Yes, the fall. Definitely the fall. Some apples here for sure.

You think again: context. Not Cunt-X this time. Cunt-text. Fear of cunt-text.

Ideas surrounding the origins of language support this. That it is not to organize any single act, or even complex series of actions — to hunt or even to gather, as previous theory would suggest — that we speak. There is no need for such complexity to accomplish tasks that wolves and apes conduct with barks and howls and gestures — but to speak of who is not there, to integrate the larger group, still an optimum at about one hundred and fifty. And that women did it first. Telling stories about each other, or the men. Something paleolinguists say they can tell from how women use language even still. The gossip theory of language it's been called. The obvious cunt-text.

Beginning with the — you call her Isis, not Eve, for the ancient Egyptian Goddess Mother of Words — of Africa. Perhaps the genetic ancestor of us all.

Then there's the men. Trying ever since to find the pure moment, the one before all those women started talking.

You will think of how in so many contexts, story, seen as gossip, the romance, has been designated undignified, lower class — female. Especially if it attempted to wrest truth from received fiction. No matter what its form. Mythological or psychological. Or concrete, like the palace walls.

You will go back to *The Tale of Genji* — no begat at all, but acknowledged as the first — or perhaps it is the first great — novel ever written. In Japanese syllabics. Which a Japanese student in one of your ESL classes once told you, the noblemen at that time would not touch. Recording was for record keepers, and as for their artistic writings — the visual characters brought from China were just so much more elegant. Even Murasaki Shikibu, the name given to the writer of *The Genji* described the court men and, for that matter, women, the most well-connected of them in any case, proving themselves in both the beauty of their calligraphy, and the elegance of their ephemeral poems — their living in the moment. While she lived — a poor relation invited to court simply for this — by telling the stories behind such moments. Another one who told to live, if not survive.

Her job was the weaving of context. For those women in love with tales and their telling, and risking syllabics to tell them, at least in their women's world. While in the introduction to the new, complete, modern translation, the Western literary critic — English, you are sure — breathes a sigh of relief, at how this passion for story-telling, well, it kept the women busy, did not let them indulge in the far more dangerous narrative of "harem politics" — that behind the scenes manipulation of the affairs of state, so common, and so disconcerting, to the British of their later empire.

Sort of like watching soap operas: In this case story-telling, for the female, better, at least, than creating the stories to tell by letting their narrative talent push those around them into action.

This is when your reality will shift. When again, you will be overwhelmed by another place, another time. As you acknowledge that this story too, as so often stories do, even those with no aim create concrete results, has created something in you. Has recontextualized itself from inside that place where narrative is not chronology but circle and spiral and ellipse that is and is and is still.

But there is no tenderness in this seduction. Because you will know suddenly why it is not the Bible or Chilam Balaam or the Popol Vuh or Gilgamesh or Beowolf or the Iliad or the Kelevala or any other early epic that has come into your mind. But this novel. Only this one. With the man in his kimono which might be a bathrobe in a palace that is a bedroom with a gas fireplace and the echo. From outside of time. A cunt-textualization. From one woman to another: *Lolita* was published the summer I turned eleven, turned into: The Genji Monagatori was written in the eleventh century.

Because it was perhaps there, in some strange anti-chronological narrative time warp, that Lolita told herself. Where Murasaki Shikibu intervenes in that story — Lolita's story — and changes it.

And opens another kind of parenthesis, only now being closed.

This story will give comfort to you. Even there, at the conference, this secret deeply held will sing to you, almost like a lullaby. Murasaki Shikibu knows, Murasaki Shikibu knows, a comfort to both your anger and your shame at your inability to overcome that wish to sulk as you say: *Lolita* was published the summer I turned eleven.

As you let the appropriate moment for any intervention pass, still, it is glorious to know that this woman, right there at the beginning of the novel, would have understood. She, and her readers, for whom the female was so clearly at the centre of the tale. Determining the context. The cunt-text. Her cunt-text determining the context. The world, the way you can see it today, the sharp closing parenthesis as women start once more to speak this story among so many others, a story we are telling. Rather than painting with your prick and writing with your balls.

It won't matter that you haven't found your own story. That yours still splits, breeds, bifurcates, dissolves into fragmented voices. For the moment it will be enough that this story is out there. That someone has told it. The way it will allow you to tell that one small part of yours. Acknowledge that anger you have felt so long. You will need only to know how Murasaki Shikibu told her world into being. Blooming forth from almost a thousand years ago to echo to that girl in the kitchen, that woman at the conference table, to tell her world. *The Tale of Genji* was written in the eleventh century will open the parenthesis that ends in your kitchen with *Lolita* was published the summer I turned eleven. Even if it will not locate the man in the bathrobe.

It will be a small story among so many that Murasaki Shikibu already knew. That still stand today, each one as one of the great stories, the ones we still tell, present always in story time — forever telling forever told. With all the emotions that go with them: Sorrow, joy, embarrassment, shame, betrayal, loss, grief, envy, jealousy, greed, desire. Stories of sexual liaisons and unrequited love, change of social station and the pride that will not admit it, illegitimacy — of any kind — and the fear of exposure, wild triumph and terrible defeat, told and retold.

While among them — and this is what you will think of that day as you look out at that audience and think your childish *Lolita* thought — there is this one. Tucked in between the rest, hidden away in some corner — perhaps of a grey room — to only recently be told again. A story that will help you to define that kitchen in which your Jane shrinks, finding her way back to her own greyness. As the men will poke and prod and later, armed with *Lolita*, call her — call you — a nymphet. After all, Nabokov was hardly the first to encounter a seductive pubescent child, or De Sade to form his wards as he would want them. A story acted out as it is told — oh, surely, this narrative is not chronological — like a play, again and again, with the permission given to perform it, that exact way, by its power as the only acknowledged version.

The way it was performed in your kitchen.

Some might argue the story's exact position in the myths of patriarchy, but few would fail to acknowledge it. You will see it as foundational, necessary, even central to male myths of love and the self. Central, perhaps, even to his being, to his coming into being, to the construction of the male gender as we know it. Where the most privileged male gets to bring up, to form, the younger bright or beautiful but powerless female — Pygmalion it is — in his image of perfect woman. And then to have her. Never to be given away. Or for that matter given a way, that is not his. While only the less privileged males will have to accept females formed by other men.

The more respectable of these stories will start, of course, when she is an older student, even a child of the streets longing for more, and will be very precise about exactly what it is, in terms of grace or power or creativity, that the liaison has given her. Even if they might exaggerate her innocence or her youth, the way Alfred Stieglitz would call the fully formed and intellectually astute thirty-year-old Georgia O'Keeffe, the Great Child, or the Surrealists search for their child goddesses among women in their forties. While in the more pornographic tales, the central pornographic tales, it is always a ward who is brought up, usually from before puberty, and it is sex she is made expert in, and pleasing the man, whoever that may be. Later she will become mistress or lover, or — since there is no blood relationship — at the last, wife. Though even those tales will seldom dare to let that girl be an actual daughter.

It will fall to her to tell him how she appreciates what he has done, whispering to him again and again how he has perfected her. Telling him how she loves it, how every day in every way he makes her better and better. The way Woody Allen says Soon Yi Previn felt. The route Anaïs Nin took. The one Virginia Woolf did not.

You will think about this. You remember the biography from the seventies that implied that if only she'd gone along with — was it a half-brother or a cousin — when he accosted her, she would have been a far better writer. Less inhibited, more free — perhaps be as gutsy as Joyce or Lawrence. Her insistence on autonomy, those critics would have it, stunted her growth; it was not one of the reasons for it. And all of it, of course, kept her unable to enjoy sex. Which was defined, for the female, until recently, simply as a matter of giving in. Of allowing yourself to be made. In more ways than one.

In contrast to such frigidity, Woody Allen would report the many improvements in Soon Yi. It gave her far greater confidence in her dealings with men, this intercourse with her mother's long-term lover. What stepfathers, and guardians, and fathers, and others, too, uncles and cousins and long-time family friends — many around you certainly did — have said again and again: That sex with them improved her character, let her discover her true sexual self, gave her — and you will be back to your Scheherazade — a way to be so very good with men, found her one thousand and one ways to manipulate them, to give them always what they wanted. And get what she did. Except that she would no longer know what that was because she could no longer be herself in the world. Have the world she tells be her own. Though perhaps there might be a private — and perhaps prosperous — one she could still retire to. Where, after all, living, not telling, well would still be the best revenge.

To validate herself she might come to believe and need the story. So that perhaps she will pass it on, too. Until it might become central to women's story, to the construction of the female as well — to acknowledge that such passivity is the centre of women's sexuality. The way for years women believed that if they accepted their femininity and were never aggressive they might achieve the better quality — and mature — vaginal orgasm.

In such a version of the story it might even be the mother who quite righteously pimps her daughter, then congratulates her on how, through one of the mother's men, she has attained her mastery of technique. It wouldn't matter, either, if the women — or even the men — believed the story completely. Part of their hearts could refuse it, even as you did back then. Because, as with so many stories that are not examined, or deconstructed, they would believe they were wrong, and still try to live it: To conform their living to it. Convinced that it was the right one. And they were wrong to complain. The way it is so embarrassing to think, as if it mattered, *Lolita* was published the summer I turned eleven.

You remember, too, how you went along once. See how your anger and your resentment reside there. As you see how you smiled at those men in that kitchen, believing that was what you were destined for and acting it sometimes: The last cajoling seductive voice that will demand to be written to determine the centre of your story. Or finding the only way to determine yourself inside that raging voice, by refusing a body and demanding to be an angel, or a man.

Later you would even listen — it was the sixties after all — and nod, to those with claims to loving, or at least having sex with, girls or boys many years under age, or family members. It is the last taboo, they would say, and like all taboos must be broken, their eyes telling you, sharp, waiting, not oblique like at the conference, that the women who would say no to it, would be broken too. Called frigid. Like Virginia Woolf. Silly. Inhibited. Like the members of Temperance Unions. Obviously unable to be truly free. Or creative. Obviously too small-minded for that. The mocking smiles silencing any woman's attempt to say that what she is protesting is her own captivity. The fact that — in analogy to the loss of voice you have just been discussing — neither women nor girls are the ones to make the decisions. Or the statements. That as women they stand against this rapacious greed that claims the souls of women as well as their bodies. That they stand for the right to autonomy, to sexuality and its expression, returned to the self. The female self. As a woman might say, too, that the question has never been sin, nor crime against property, but violation of trust. Of the essence of the separate self. Just as Murasaki Shikibu protests.

It does not take up much space, this story in the Genji. It even makes you wonder if there might be others like Murasaki Shikibu who have had the opportunity to speak, at least quietly, the way she wrote her story into those belittled syllabics, where only the women would hear, or look. Perhaps if you looked carefully you might find other, small, denigrated worlds men would not enter ready, shouting, to change her version. Her world. Stories hidden away in some corner, the way in the Genji that story is hidden among kimonos and coloured paper and perfume. You even wonder if, in the abridged translations, this story appears at all.

It is a startling, a perfect, aside. As perfect, as sharp, as brilliant, as the one that pens the red-nosed princess forced to keep up appearances in a house far too cold. You remember shivering when you read that. A shiver again, when you read this: The description of the nuptial ceremony the beautiful and brilliant Prince Genji has planned for his wife-to-be. The one — and, oh, there were many pages given to his search for the perfect woman — Prince Genji took from her widowed grandmother at the age of — what was it — eight or ten, per- haps eleven: The author's namesake, Murasaki. Who perhaps the author identified with, naming her so, we will never know, unsure as we are even of the lady's identity, much less her reasons for being at court. Except that she tells so well that some speculate it was this and this alone that brought her there: That she could make the world with her telling.

   With this other little Murasaki, the one Prince Genji is about to turn from his daughter — for yes, he had her call him Father — into his wife. When in two brief sentences Lady Murasaki Shikibu tells us how Little Murasaki had not dreamed he had anything of the sort on his mind. That she feels herself a fool, to repose her whole confidence in so gross and unscrupulous a man. And so very simply is the beautiful Genji, the perfect courtier, brought low. Whom throughout the novel you have been forced to admire, as above the common lot of men. This, his young daughter-wife's opinion of him.

It will never be retracted. Even as she learns to behave as her new husband wishes.

You breathe deeply each time you read it. Even, your hand shakes. As you feel it echoing down the centuries. Lady Murasaki Shikibu penning in one instant, for her namesake Murasaki, the feelings of women around the world, eyes down, behaviour perfect, hearts aching through the years.

You know that ache of unforgivable betrayal. A pain, red in the belly, that makes you limp, unsure of the ground beneath you, caused by one you thought so close to you, that only your good could be in his mind. You have felt this more than once, with more than one in whom you had placed a daughterly trust. Wanting, always desperately — it was seductive of you wasn't it — to trust. Like Little Murasaki, her naive trust, half her charm. And the other half, her demure and sullen rebellion. Like yours. Taking yourself away from them in that kitchen even as they spoke of *Lolita*.

You hear it. Feel it. A blow to the chest from a thousand years ago. The simplicity of this woman's story. And how, for this moment, this brief episode, it is not Genji, not the Prince, but little Murasaki at the centre of the tale.

You will learn too, how quickly Little Murasaki's feelings were suppressed. For her place at court. The way you still repress yourself, your earnestness, your desire to cry out. For your place in this new court, your place in the debate. And just the same. You, Little Murasaki: Sullen, intense, demure. As you learned to go along. You wonder now if Lady

Murasaki, having found her place in court, told and told, just to get Little Murasaki back.

For you, only the intensity remains. Though you have learned to cover it with a loud laugh instead of with the back of your hand.

At the conference table, and often after, you will imagine it. All those elegant women listening in their beautiful kimonos as Lady Murasaki paints with words kimonos even more beautiful. Shows off the elegance of the paper and ink her characters might choose to listeners well versed in the elegance of paper and ink, even in the ephemeral poems left about as messages for friends or lovers. Their language only slightly less magnificent than the teller's — they had invited her to court for her greater eloquence, after all — or her characters'.

You will know that they can hear it. These brilliant, elegant women of the court can hear it. Feel it squirm into their guts. Where they could never scream it out anymore than you can. It will hit them, like you, in that hidden place beyond elegance or even aesthetics, beyond the form of the tale well told. In that same place inside you from which those words wished to pop out.

You hear it again. Feel it. That hidden betrayal. That hidden shame. That can build selves as elegant and changing, as elusive and fluid, as seductive, as that court world. The selves that you know so well. The one that smiles and goes to ground. Another that holds you against the voices, refusing to let them dissolve you. But that still refuses to hear them or to be the teller in your tale. That prefers, always, elegance to truth: Appearance to having to say who you are. Anything to having to acknowledge the shame that has made you. To having to tell it in order to make your world: The one in which you can be you.

You will lean back, close your eyes, breathe. Watch the clock approach eleven, the end of the session. While those two statements will stand there in your mind like monuments to the place of telling. *Lolita* was published the summer I turned eleven. *The Tale of Genji* was written in the eleventh century. A set of brackets contextualizing you. Cunttextualizing you. Together pushing you toward another story. Or another parenthesis in your story. With luck, another episode. Until perhaps you can find the teller at the centre of your tale. Declare, with your son: The world is a story I am telling.

((( )))

It will seem wrong somehow. Just that little bit off no matter what you do. Until that day in the restaurant again. The same restaurant. Only this time it will not be a luncheon in the middle of a conference, but you, alone, meeting one old friend.

You have continued to go there. Refusing to be intimidated by the floor tiles, or the large planes of lath, their plaster removed. The water damage of the old fire, or a carpenter creating a safe urban look. A look of damage, a look of safe damage, an oxymoronic look, you think, giggling, stepping resolutely over the floor tiles, to the security of the scratched up wood floor behind.

You can't even imagine the intent. Except you love it, take a strange damaged joy in this pastiche yourself.

You will tell the friend of the floor tiles. How they have taken you into that terrible grey place, where you cannot find the pathway out. How it just seems one long, long hallway. Your life perhaps, a long grey hallway. But even then, despite the aching, the almost constant aching, you will know you are putting a good face on it. Making it personable.

Perhaps you need to. Perhaps it is part of that safe cupola room. That if you smile this way, sophisticated, discuss it in this tone of voice, it will be like those Fridays your mother's Manhattan woman friend, wife of a *New Yorker* editor, would take you after school, buy you a small Steiff toy. And you, safe, your hand in hers. Perhaps this is what you are doing for Jane. Convincing her the world is safe. Even with floor tiles. You are here to tell her so. Perhaps that too, the joy in the damaged walls.

Only you think there is more. That it is something else, too. Something about pleasure in pain. Something you have not yet understood. The seductive voice you vaguely discern calling to the angry one. Both of them taking joy in hurt. The way you sometimes do, cutting along your arms with exacto knives. Something else you do not understand.

You will look at the glint off your own knife. And the food on your plate, recently arrived, will call to you. You will slide the food back and forth, examining the bright red of the tomato salsa, the dark coagulating crimson of the bloody meat you have cut into. Lamb chops, medium rare, your favourite. Something in it will tell you the story you have just constructed, all of it, Genji, Scheherazade, the incestuous family, something in it does not ring true. Or fails to ring true for you. You have borrowed a stereotype, or perhaps just a metanarrative, the way so much story does, a way to fit yourself to the narrative, to find a place for yourself, rather than to find your narrative, the truth of what has made you.

You will hear a voice then. A real voice. Not the flat disembodied voice of delirium but the kind that makes you turn around, sure the speaker is there. This happens sometimes, though, thankfully, not often. Liar, liar, pants on fire, it repeats.

You try to silence it, stabbing at the meat. Only to find that your flesh. Along your arms your legs your back your stomach. Your flesh seems to burn. And there is that painful pleasure again. What, you ask yourself, what? What after all, could be untrue?

What here, could violate your story? Not Murasaki's, but your own.

Is it something in that accusation, Liar, liar pants on fire, or is it in that burning in your pants?

You will continue to play with your food. Pushing it back and forth on the plate, without lifting your fork. You will look the way you did in your early adolescence. You are aware of it in your body. You feel displaced, the way you sometimes do at night. You are sure the Little Lady Murasaki looked just so as she examined her nuptial sweets: her betrayal. Probably pushed them back and forth too, at least nudged them, with her chopsticks. The way you look, only you do not know what it is, at that betrayal in the food.

Demure they always called you. Back then. Demure. Looking down. In pale pastels. Such a contrast with the bright weaving you now so often wear.

You do remember one dress. How you loved it. A blue and white checked silk shirtwaist, its collar buttoned high. You can even smell the copper of the braided silver dipped head-band you wore with it, that cost you a dollar, and placed black stains onto the tips of the white cloth gloves your aunt bought you each Easter. You remember too, the small square silk handkerchief you tied around the ponytail you were so proud of, when, finally, you had been allowed to grow your hair. It, too, cost a dollar.

So many things you had that cost a dollar. A dollar three,

with the tax. That you bought with the money your aunt sent you each time you wrote her. A dollar a letter was the rule. Each item, mostly a collection of handkerchief-sized scarves and headbands, a mark of the innocent femininity you thought would bring safety as well as adulthood. You remember, too, how skinny you were — today they might even call you anorexic. As you tried to be that dress, those gloves, that thin woven band. Just those, the accoutrements of femininity, nothing more. As you attempted to escape your body. Adulthood, without a body, your greatest ambition.

You will find yourself moving the food on your plate back and forth faster and faster. You are surprised by your own vehemence, know that you must stop. You are afraid you will be caught. That others in the restaurant will wonder about you. Your anger. That you will be punished. It doesn't matter that you know no one there has that power over you.

Your response will bring tears of rage to your eyes.

Once more, you are sure you do not want to keep doing this. Worrying at your stories, at your story, the way you do at your food. The only problem is: You no longer know how to stop. Don't know if there is a way to stop. Because there is only this. Thinking and drawing. The rest is pain. Pain that drives you by moments, far too many moments, to contemplate suicide. And to stop yourself the way alcoholics who go to AA must stop themselves from having a drink. By counting the minutes you can postpone the act. Knowing you are better when it is hours you can make yourself think of waiting.

Right now you are actively stopping yourself from stabbing the back of your hand with your fork. You do know you don't want to be here. Not in this restaurant, not in this strange netherworld you have come to inhabit. Not in this life you've been given. And know no more of a way to escape it than you did when the abuse happened. When you did not want to be there either. All you know how to do is pretend you are somewhere else. Pretend you are someone else.

You decide you will take a deep breath and go back to building Jane's safe room at the top of her building, above the rotting smells of the Gowanus Canal. Maybe you will tell your friend about it. Or about how you have been constructing a new story for Scheherazade, an academic treatise on Murasaki Shikibu.

You take one last angry swipe at your food. As if to punish it. Moving between the bright red of the salsa to the dark crimson of the bloody meat. What is it about these favourite foods, red meat and tomatoes, that today make you so furious?

You gasp.

Speechless, you reach for your throat. Your windpipe again. You gesture absently at your plate, at what is on it, then gesture a trip to the washroom with your hands. Your friend is shocked by the look on your face, equally shocked by what your plate contains. Though she must think it strange. This is not the usual way you react to things like this. She knows they are a strangely twisted part of your life. This friend was with you for a ladybug crawling out of your lettuce in mid-February. Don't kill it, she'd said to the waiter, it has to have come all the way from Mexico. She's been around for the jokes about free dinners. Even laughed with you when you said that maybe it was good you'd never met Julio Cortázar — the one writer you'd ever really wanted to meet — since he was phobic about encountering such things. So why is she doing this, your friend must be thinking. What is this fear? This flight?

By the time you get back from the washroom, she will know. She has poked through the salsa with her own fork and seen it there. It is easy to understand someone's fear about this. Had you not been playing, had you not seen it, had you put the salsa into your mouth and swallowed.

She, too, will break out into a sweat. Understand your pallor.

But you will know more. And it will not just be about what could have happened but about what did. Somehow, in that gleaming staple there on the plate, there among the red meat and tomatoes, gleaming its industrial steel gleam, you will see the closing of a parenthesis.

Another parenthesis.

As if your world had been held forever there. The brutal closing of the throat around that steel bracket: The Parenthesis of Red Meat and Tomatoes.

You will not know it then, what it is. Not really. It won't be that kind of resolution. Like a quick movie on multiple per-sonality disorder — dissociative identity disorder they call it today. Oh, my god, I remember now — as if you'd misplaced your keys or glasses — and it's done.

It will just be that you perceive a road hidden there. As if in some form of strange symbolic universe you have had to walk into this restaurant, over the floor tiles, by the bare lath, to encounter this: A summary of your story on your plate.

You will not try to explain. Just accept the free bottle of red wine you are being offered, drink it with your friend and be done. But your mind will be in another place, home with Jane, home in your attic room, in the turret room you have invented for her.

You will know now why it is Scheherazade who fascinates you. Why you have been so busy building variants. And because, suddenly, you know how the pieces fit together, it does not matter if they don't always fit you.

Because what you will see that staple do, that staple square as a bracket that adds or subtracts from a text, is the closing of the first parenthesis in your life, one that lasted almost two years, one at whose end, you got up from the bed in your mother's room and promised, promised and promised, to eat red meat and tomatoes. The way you have always eaten red meat and tomatoes, loved red meat and tomatoes. Red meat and tomatoes and spinach and liver and all those other items containing iron. And while spinach was always Popeye and your dad, red meat and tomatoes were the promise of a complicity you only now begin to understand.

The bracket between the last time you saw Mark Murphy, long before he went to Africa to die, and the day you got up from a bed where you had been confined with anemia.You always seemed so active, your mother would say, we just didn't notice until you collapsed. And while the medicine on your bed will tell you it was much more than this, much more extreme, still, anemia has always plagued you. And the promise to eat all those good things, all those iron-containing things, was a promise made to avoid the daily needles, the sharp glinting metal and glass of the needles, that have left you still with what is almost a phobia, unable, except with extreme effort to even take a blood test, much less give blood.

Except you always thought it was just a matter of days. And the hallucinated feeling of that room just a matter of the medicine, of the illness. You did not know that it was almost two years, or that the promise to be good, was a promise of silence. This is why your terrified recoil at that sharp square instrument, used to seal the packing crates of tomatoes coming up from Mexico or California. This is the location of the terrible centre of your tale that is not a teller, but an act of scattering.

Yes, Mom, I will be good Mom, I'll eat them all Mom, always contained something else, something else that was in that room. At first so frightening that for days you will be so immobilized that you will attempt to renew your promise, taking to your bed just as you did with the anemia. And you will know that what you had promised then, as you attempt to promise the same to Jane now, is a forgetting.

Because the truth that will be within your reach will break even your promise to her: that the cupola you have built will be safe.

You will find yourself promising over and over to be good. Promising yourself, promising Jane, you will be good, you will be good and forget it, the sense of hurt, the sense of betrayal, the sense that you have been split open split apart, scattered like ashes to the four winds — you were no more than five — by the horror of the abuse, the horror that can still overcome you looking down, looking at food, that will overcome you this day in the restaurant.

The grey silencing metal like the grey silence of that space in which you have walked so long. The space from which Jane speaks, even as you try to find your way back to her. Drawing her, as you have done, at the barred downstairs window of your mother's house, and silent always silent those times you are able to draw her into the attic room. And there so often as you curl up to sleep at night, trying to be in her cupola with her, there is, instead, the dark parenthesis, the whirling vortex that you do not know how you enter, but from which you cannot exit, glinting grey blue grey green steel grey in the blood red pain of your days: Your silence.

And tales of a nurturing that never happened, that you nonetheless told yourself was there with each bite. They really care about me, you said, and hid your story between the parentheses of your teeth, between bite and bite. Delicate bites because you gag so easily. Your throat ready always to close around the staple. Around the truth that will tear it apart. While your story hides. Inside. Untold.

You become afraid you are doing to Jane what was done to you. By repeating those stories of the nurturing that never was. Even as you feel how you do it in your mother's voice. You can feel how the words, or more than the words, the tone, go deeper than you thought. Grab at something you still deny. Because your family will never have been that one you have described. Even if the betrayal was there.

It was other. What was hidden in your words of rage. That you have always rejected, preferring inarticulate pain to knowledge. Moving away from that voice to leave Jane in her grey cell. Or sitting on her stair half-way up and half-way down, frozen by the more horrific betrayal that lies still silenced beneath any story you can make up and say. Even the one you made for Little Murasaki.

For the longest time you cannot begin to tell it. Though you can feel its edges. There is so much in it of how history works. And context. Pain begetting pain, and betrayal, betrayal. Those schooled in self-hatred bringing it to bear against those like them. Your mother's hatred of herself acted out on your body. As you find yourself thinking that you have even grasped onto the power of the image of the typical patri-archal family in feminism, with its absolute rule by the father, the one so many books say are the kind to beget incest, to release yourself from your memories. From your need, and your duty, to look at your whole story, and to look at her. At her. To see her. That in looking for male abusers — and they have been there — the obvious centre of your choking suffo-cating terror has been passed by. And only now will you learn that many women have done the same. Those who make up male abusers. Because they have been told it cannot happen, because they cannot believe it of someone so like them, they cannot admit being abused by a woman. The threat to identity is too great.

You are sure now that you will find it: Your own story. Its centre so long the missing core of the action. It does not matter that it will be found much later. As for now the stories will continue to polyp off and multiply, split and recombine. As your throat aches. And you wish for a teller to make your world. To find the teller who makes your world.

What will change is your confidence. Moments of despair turn to days of exhausting work. At the end of which you know will be a birth. Thoughts of suicide, too, are less frequent. And more peripheral. As if the act were among many displayed to choose from. And the choice was yours.

You will look at the staple, remember the days in bed, the blood tests and the hopelessness, the desperate grey days before you had taken to your bed. Still, it will be a long time before you can see that last grey gleaming bracket in your salsa as the closing of the parenthesis in which you have been caught, Jane has been caught. You will still feel your throat closing each time as you decide to speak.

And it is only later, much later, that you will find the man you have hunted. The one who caused that rage. When you have faced your mother and named her, not as complicit but as principle in your abuse — what she did to you, what she had the men do to you — it will only be then that he will appear. The one who stood, first, in the long line of male abusers, who gently persuaded then used you. Giving rise, for the first time, to the feelings. Because there were others, some long remembered — you did become a seductive little girl, after all, a perfect nymphet, who at least one man would betray in her early adolescence, those *Lolita* years, when they all examined you. But there were few you trusted enough for their acts to be named betrayal. With this one not a stepfather but a father figure, someone who'd been around a lot, maybe doing it with your mother too. And for you much like Genji, waiting and attempting to form you, he was a sailor, too, like your dad, though he'd gone back to university, telling you stories, tall tales of his own adventures and Norse mythology — *The Tale of Baldur*, he did give you that. But who said he would wait and marry you, and then, one day when you were fourteen, him married and you running away from home, when you needed a check cashed he decided you should suck his cock. Bringing to the surface an anger so startling, your hands shook as you imagined yourself stabbing him with the gravity knife he'd given you to carry. The pain and anger, so lightning bright because you had forgotten it was there.

So that it is not that one you will discover. But the first. The one to arouse such memories of seduction and betrayal that you would claim to wait for him forever on your stair. That one. Who you will only come to know years later. Writing this. When mostly — and it will show in that this can be written at all, to you, my child-self growing up, becoming grown, knowing the world — the days will be clear, the sky blue, and the centre of yourself, the teller, real, discovered. With the centre of the tale. And that first red meat and tomatoes parenthesis will be closed, contained, your mother standing in its centre. Placing it in context. So that you will write the recent past speaking to the farther past, and that to an even farther one.

And it will only be then, the now of first writing that you will come to know. And May 1st, after a late-night filing of your income tax that you will start to write it. When you will remember, and — as has happened so often — say, Of course, of course. I knew that. I remember that. How could I ever have forgotten?

A whole segment of your life will then become clear. You will watch the room, see the man approaching you in the room, the man with your mother in the room, and feel again the dread of those three sections of the year, and this the worst:

Tax time. Not Mark Murphy's — that official father's — death, halfway between mid-summer and the fall equinox when, unless your dad was home, you were always home alone with your mother in Brooklyn, but the end of the long terrible yearly parenthesis — you could call it that, The Yearly Parenthesis — begun with the winter solstice and the terror that the attempted celebration of Christmas would always let into your world, and ended in early spring, when American income taxes are due. The one horror inside the year that much as it has affected you, you have refused, until now, both to remember and to deal with. When every other day — strangely enough she could never do it two days in a row — your mother would drink herself into that personality change, where she would become the unpredictable storm centre you have never been able to describe, hardly even to imagine, except as a weather system you could choose to predict if never understand. Who would offer always humiliation and abuse, making fun of you making fun of your brother, hunting you to abuse you, frenetic and wild and the next day with no memory. A cycle repeated and repeated as she would end each of her drinking days, after hours of receipts or gnashing her teeth over their lack, she would once more open the bottle of scotch. And blame you, you and your brother, for her fallen position in the world. Until there would be that day when finally the taxes would be filed. And the drinking would become less frenetic, perhaps once or twice a week, the abuse gentler. Until Christmas. Or July. When it would be at its worst again.

And sometimes there would be others. Who were there then. The friends who were not friends who helped her to file. Who urged her to drink and did things to her and with her and with you who were held there. To watch or to participate but to add some special thrill. Her joy in degradation increased by your being part of it. Her hatred of you and herself in you obvious and replete. As she would orchestrate it all.

There was one in particular. In that bright room with her. What will have kept you from dealing with your taxes, for so long. From looking at that, its horror. Even here in Canada, with filing on April 30th, weeks later. Because you could not face that howling, and that blaming, in your mind. Or what would come as a result of it. Or even face that man, your first Genji, who said he would comfort you. Much less your mother, whose culpability will always be the hardest to admit. Until that day when sitting in a small house in B.C. you will pace and pace, going from room to room, tears running down your cheeks, and then you will vomit. And then the next day, you will call an accountant.

And file on time. For the first time in over ten years.

And when you are through, write this down.

By then you will know that your mother is the figure behind your Scheherazade. The one who always told the stories different from what they were. And tore your throat, your voice, apart — then asked you to do the same. Who cleaned up the stories and polished them — or just forgot. The one who made you mistrust words, so that you could only write after moving back into English — from Julio Cortázar and your first stories in Spanish, your own second language. A language of choice, not coercion, and strangely — you will think back on the conference conversation — your dad's third language, in which he, too, felt most comfortably himself. So that for you, story will arise there, while, for the longest time, English would remain the language of the lie, of coercion — or, at its best, of plotting a getaway — or, the overthrow of a government. You still find transliterated Spanish grammar in your writing, or a proverb, a turn of phrase, as if that language taught you that subtlety as well as story was possible. The way you will wish to write how life had ceased to contain pleasure, and the words in your mind are still *ni un asomo de placer.*

You will understand, too, that while your drawings have given you, given Jane, the colours back, it is also true that they were the one place to avoid your mother, that visual world so completely your dad's, the one she never understood. That it was this gathering of strength that allowed you to see beyond her retellings. You remember how she told you you were crazy. That she couldn't possibly have done what you say she had been doing. And besides, if she had, it would affect you as much as it did her. Whether you lied about such abuse, or told the truth about it, either way it would render you so outside the norm you would be crazy. Something made clear in the structure of the house again and again. Only now you will be able to draw your way to the edge, out of the whirling vortex to where that parenthesis can be closed, safe and articulated, behind you. And then you will speak it in words. Until it will become a place you can safely visit. Because you never have to live there again.

It will be that way with your mother's house. Once you have identified her. The storyteller. Who has told over and over the stories you have believed for years. Even that your dad was not your father. Telling the events of the house into innocence and tall tales, her own adventures and discoveries, the one for whom the nights of your days never happened. As she dictated which stories could and which could not be told. Which you needed to tell and why. While it is that place you gave your Scheherazade, that typical patriarchal family, from which you suspect she comes. That she is the teller whose voice has been broken by abuse, and her own need to hide from herself, from her roles both as abused and as abuser.

Though she will never tell you. If by now, she still remembers. Anymore than she might remember what she did to you. Night after night. But you will no longer ask. Never again for another story.

They would be always the same. Whether of horseback

rides, or dances at the country club, or her adventures flying around the country as a reporter, before she fell apart. Or even of how she tried so hard to keep it together after Mark Murphy died. Or how your dad rescued her when her last shoe was broken. You will not keep that Scheherazade alive through her telling. Through her constant changing of the story. And your acknowledgement of it.

It is your time to leave. To carefully shut the door. As she tells and retells, never ending her sentences, the stories she has wanted you to hear, that she wants the world to hear, over and over to an empty house. Or one, at least, empty of you. While you will go on, making your path, your child-self held by the hand.

But this will start to happen only after you have walked a long, long road not of your choosing. In which your drawings will be your only signposts. As you will proceed in silence. Until finally you will begin for the first time to speak, not the story you were told to tell, but the one you lived. That parts of you lived. With its terrible violations of your body and of your mind. And the stories will come back, the multiplying stories, because they have found a place they come from that is you. Not just beginnings and endings and unfinished sentences like the ones your mother tells. But a story with a direction, a place to go. In the end you will find the teller at the centre of the tellers at the centre of the tale. Your tale.

You will bring her then to your cupola, bring Jane out of that grey featureless space. The one in your mother's house. In her upstairs room. You will walk with her in your mind. Out the window and onto the front stoop and down. Out the ladder onto the roof and over to the fire escape and down. Onto the drainpipe and out to the fire escape and down. Out the back door and over the fence. The routes will be clear. Story no longer a sleight of hand to confuse the hearer — or the self.

A day will come when you will do even that differently.

When you will walk boldly to the stairs and slowly down, your hand resting on the bannister like a lady's. Your head nodding to each room, acknowledging them. Your eyes tracing each nook and cranny. Until you will reach the front door. And you will open it. And you will walk out. And you will lock it behind you.

But that will be the day you write your mother, and tell her exactly what she has done. Saying you will no longer cover for her, but want acknowledgement, recognition. An accounting. An apology. And suddenly, so very suddenly, even though she will never answer directly, all the road ways will be clear. The routes in and out of her house, and your own.

But there will be one strange, final, parenthesis. You will have no idea how to title this one. Except maybe the last. The Last Parenthesis.

She will send you a letter. Not an apology, but what she has always done. The one place of your conspiracy. Teaching you joy in the outside world, in what happens there. What she has done for years, sending you clippings even when you lived in New York. From her days as a journalist she has been an inveterate clipper of newspapers. Even in the depth of her worst alcoholism, it was what connected her. And that is what this will be, this response to your challenge: A clipping from *The New York Times*.

She had already told you about it. Before your letter, in one of that last series of phone calls, Sunday morning phone calls, when she would only chat, pretending nothing else was going on, the way she always had, when she told you she was sending on a review she called brilliant, fascinating. Of a time you must remember. One of the days of implicit criticism, of why you fled New York. Why you weren't there still. To be brilliant, fascinating. But you must remember Anne Sexton, she will go on, Quite the poet, you know, well, a brilliant new biography. And then it will be there in the mail.

Not the new biography of Anne Sexton but a review of that work, in which the reviewer attempts to analyze whether this is indeed just a chance to tear apart yet another celebrity, the crazy lady who at least made good, something your mother has always told you she refused to do to Mark Murphy — and to you, she has always said — when a writer wanted to write his last days, something like *The Crack-Up*, that story of F. Scott Fitzgerald's last days with the bottle, this to be the story of Mark Murphy and how he went from being the writer who invented the classic *New Yorker* profile to a derelict in Johannesburg, the book guaranteed to make him a cult figure, the way Mia made Jim Agee. But which you think now she refused to do to herself, to have her own life closely examined. While the review you are reading will go on too, to question the ethics behind Anne Sexton's therapist's release of the tapes of her therapy.

You will note suddenly, with the same sick sensation as when you looked down at the giant staple in your salsa, there on the page, the central point to it all, the contested family secret. Not its existence, this time, but whether it should ever have been told: Anne Sexton's sexual abuse of her daughter, Linda Gray Sexton, who, in the book — you will get it after all, after this — speaks of how wonderful it was to have been brought up by so extraordinary a mother, the way Anaïs Nin might speak of her father, even if Anne Sexton did make it difficult, purposely it seemed, to determine the boundaries between them. While seeing that fact noted, before you can relent, you will crumple the clipped newsprint and burst into tears. Into relentless sobbing. The way you cried well into your twenties, when you were alone.

Then, weeks later again, you will go through a box your mother has sent you months before, perhaps more than a year, that you have opened, but avoided sorting. The way in moments of anxiety you will often do with your mail. A box full of trendy second-hand clothes and folk art redolent with the oil furnace odour of New York basements, accompanied by the inevitable articles from *The New York Times*, and the *New Yorker*, *New York Magazine* and *Esquire*, or maybe *Vanity Fair*, or *The Village Voice*. While as you tentatively sort this bunch of clippings with your hand, conscious of the old paper smell that always marked her house, it will be there too. Among the old newsprint and the wools of the same colour. Forgotten again by both of you.

That same review.

This time you will not crumple it. You will put it in the same file where you have put the letter of farewell that you have sent her. And you will laugh then and wonder.

What part of her was it, that made her send this, you will ask yourself. Send it twice. At first you will think it was just what she had always done. A reminder, even a panicked reminder, sending it twice like that, that you owed her silence for what she had given you. A bit too much like red meat and tomatoes. But then you will think again. Of the first copy, never mentioned, there amid all those old yet lovely clothes. Sent, perhaps even a year before, when all your mother knew was that you had entered therapy.

What magic place in the mystery of identity had that come from, you will ask. It will seem then like a secret message. Something your Scheherazade might send out about the truth of her relationship with the sultan, or Murasaki — either Murasaki — telling Genji into the future. Why else would your mother send you a review of a biography in which its subject — a mother — sexually abuses her daughter, written by a poet neither of you had spent much time on. Was it the child Mickey reaching out to the child you, to your Jane, from some secret hidden place of her own? Or was it that mother who truly wished to nurture you, no matter what horrors she created by night?

In the end you will simply put it away. Filed among so many other voices and remnants from the years just past. As you will return yourself to the centre of your tale, your on-going tale, this now just a small piece of its setting. And you will turn to your son, seven now, and laugh with him, and even if he doesn't say it anymore, you will know that the world, your world, is now a story you are telling. You, the teller at its centre.

And yet you will treasure this last parenthesis. Among all the parentheses. Think of the two copies of the review as if they were the brackets that began and ended this year of draw-ing, as you return once more to words. And besides, you will think, this is likely as close to an apology as you will ever get.

And, perhaps, as close to forgiveness as you will ever come.

THE ANGEL KEVIN:
FOR THE CAUSE OF LIBERTY

Don't ask me who I am because I won't answer. I'll tell you what you can call me, though. Kevin. You can call me Kevin. Because I sing the song. If you want to know more about me, I'll just tell you this: I'm the secret. I'm the one who waits.

She doesn't know it. Only I do. I know I'm waiting. I even know what for. I hum it under my breath sometimes. While I wait. I imagine it sometimes. Vivid pictures. While I wait. I'm the secret. That's me. That's all I'll tell you. Don't ask again. Call me Kevin. That's it.

She doesn't know how much she owes me. With her little dances and her little songs. None of those kids do. Or how much they'll owe me later. They have no idea. They just sit around, and enjoy the sun. And their little games.

Sometimes she plays patty cake. But it's always by herself. That's funny to watch. The hands reaching up to clap thin air. It's not her fault she has no other little girls to play with. The good mothers won't let their girls play with her, and the boys wouldn't play that game, even if they knew how. Anymore than they would skip rope.

That's something she can do by herself. But it's not the same. Even if she imagines herself in dresses with long braids instead of my short hair and blue jeans. While she sings those silly songs about silly things. Like being a pretty little Dutch girl, and how all the boys around the block are crazy over her.

Maybe they are. Or maybe she's crazy over them, it's hard to tell. They're the only ones who'll play with her. I think that's okay. At least it's okay for me. But she does things with them. Things the other little girls won't do. Wiggling and strutting and taking off all her clothes. And letting them look down there. Just like her mother.

I guess she's my mother, too. Only I won't call her that. I won't say Mom, oh Mom, I love you Mom. Even when she's nice. When she isn't drinking and there are no men around, I won't say that. I just call her Liz, after the actress. The one with all the husbands. Or Lizzie. Because she's not beautiful like the actress. And she doesn't have class. I don't think the real Liz's lipstick gets smeared all over her chin. And I'm sure she doesn't drink and sing, rrrr rrrr rrrr.

You see, I won't make up to people just to be nice. The way she does to our mother. To Lizzie. Or to the boys. Tell them I love them. Or always try to do what they want. Not ever. That's not the way I am. I wait. And I watch. For the moment to make my move. No one would call me Honey, the way they do her. No one would dare call me that. She deserves that name. Honey, Bunny, sweet as Honey. I call her that, too.

She does like honey. It's her favourite. On bread. There were even these boys once who told her they would cover her in it. You do what we want or we'll cover you in honey, and put you with the ants, in the anthill. They sang at her. And danced around in a circle. It's the only time I've seen boys do that, except when they play Indians.

All Honey could think to do was giggle. What do you want, she said. What do you want me to do? And she smiled and she shook her head and she opened her mouth and she looked just like Lizzie. Especially when she started to feel it down there between her legs, the way she sometimes does, the way Lizzie must. Oh, cover me in honey, she said, again. Honey loves honey. Cover me in honey. Only you can lick it off. But that's not what they wanted. They wanted something else. Something much worse. And she smiled at that too. And the honey oozed out.

I didn't smile. I wanted to get her, then, I really did. And them, too. Those are the times I won't wait. When she gets so incredibly stupid she has no idea what she's getting into. I just act. I balled her up into a fist. Her whole body one big fist. And I exploded. From inside her body. Where I wait. Her hands and her feet and her teeth suddenly pouncing to do exactly what I wanted.

Because I'm her secret. The one you'll never really know. Anymore than they'll ever threaten to cover anyone in honey after what I did to them. One by one. Even to her. I hurt her. Let her body get all covered in bruises. She didn't have to want that honey. To feel it on her body.

Then when Lizzie asked her what happened, she just whimpered and said: They were mean to me. Mom, those boys were mean to me. And Lizzie took her in her arms, and said something about boys. How she had to stop playing with boys, or pretending she was a boy. I don't remember. Something like that.

Lizzie's breath was already beginning to smell, that sweet smell it gets when she drinks, and when she hugged Honey I could feel her breasts, the ones she lets the men play with. I wanted to be sick then. So I stopped listening to the two of them. And just sang my song. It's the only song I know. But it's worth more than all the stupid childish songs Honey sings. More than Lizzie's song. That voice like the

needle at the end of the record, repeating, rrrr rrrr rrrr. It's
the song my father taught me before he left. It's a grown-up
song. About important things. Heroes. And great deeds. The
kind I wait to do. I ran off into a corner and sang it. And
didn't hear Lizzie at all.

Early on a Monday morning
In a lonely prison cell
British soldiers tortured Barry
For the things he would not tell

Sometimes I sing Kevin instead of Barry. Though it's
really the same. Kevin Barry. I just like Kevin better. It doesn't
sound like the name of a man who might come to the house.
It sounds good, and noble. Like an angel. I use that name
because I know all about torture.

They do torture Honey sometimes. Those boys practice
on her. No matter how much she smiles or tells them not to
do it, at least not to tie her up. She'll do whatever they want
if they don't tie her up, they don't have to tie her up since she
loves to do what they want. This time she'll do even more if
they don't tie her up, and she giggles and licks her lips. And
it's her turn to wait. With that feeling down there that she
likes so much just growing and growing. Until she finds out
what they want this time.

She got caught once, doing that. With one of the boys in
the bathroom. Near the toilet with the old wooden tank, way
up high with its pull-string. She was pulling the boy's string.
At least that's what he said, laughing. Pull my string.

Lizzie chased the boy away and said he would never be
allowed in the house again if he ever did anything like that,
and comforted Honey and patted her and hugged her and
asked her to tell Lizzie if any of those nasty boys ever did
anything like that ever again. And Honey cried those great
big blubbery little girl tears, not like the tears I cry, not at all,
the ones the anger pushes out, all over my face; while Lizzie
wrapped Honey in her arms, and called her Honey, my little

Honey Bunch, and said it again: You shouldn't be playing with boys. Something like that. Nice girls don't play with boys. And didn't she want to be a nice little girl?

And then Lizzie asked her if any of them had ever done anything like that before, anything at all. And Honey just shook her head. Shook it and shook it. At least she was that smart. But Lizzie still sent her to her room to take her time to remember. Just in case Lizzie said. Just in case.

If I get anything to say about it, I let them tie Honey up. And pretend to torture her, at least a little. It's her brother and that one friend who do it, and they're the ones who mean her the least harm. They're her buddies. Like in the war games they play. I think that maybe that way, she'll learn. Not to smile like that.

And besides. It's hard being tortured. And she's got to learn to take it. Honey doesn't really understand that. But it's why I let them do it to her. Why I don't make her fight back all the time. I think if they do it enough she'll understand. How to resist it. How to be brave. How not to knuckle under and beg. I just keep hoping the boys will help teach her how it all works.

Like being sent to her room. That's being held in solitary. When they wait for you to go crazy and spill the beans. And being trapped upstairs while Lizzie and the men are drinking downstairs, that's being held prisoner. Under threat of more torture. Like the men coming into her room, to do things with her like they do with Lizzie. Threats are torture. And Honey doesn't feel the same way about the men as she does about the boys. She really is afraid of them.

And she doesn't know that if you're a prisoner, even when they're nice, it's still torture. Because the threat is always there. That they'll take the niceness all away again if you don't cooperate. And it hurts much worse than if you'd never believed them. Never had any niceness at all.

It's like the good cop and the bad cop in the movies. One

promises you things, and the other hurts you or calls you names or tells you the awful things they're going to do to you. And then when you cooperate they do it anyway. And that hurts worse than anything. Like they're laughing at you. Like kids saying nya-nya-nyanyanya and holding something you want so bad just out of reach. I get into a lot of fights over things like that. And mostly I win. It doesn't matter how big the other kid is, that's how mad I am.

Like that time with Lizzie. All that syrupy language. All that, Oh you poor baby. All that, Tell me all about it. When Honey almost did. Until I made her sing my song. Over and over. In the corner of her room.

Names of all his brave companions
Other things they wished to know
Turn informer and we'll free you
Barry proudly answered: No

And the next thing you know, there was Lizzie drinking again. She got to play both cops that time. The sober cop and the drunk cop. With the drunk cop yelling at Honey and threatening her. What a disgraceful dirty little girl she was. Dirty. A little cunt. A little cunt. A stupid little cunt. What did she expect if she was always rubbing her cunt in the boys' faces. What did she expect? Maybe now she wanted to do it with the men, too. Lizzie was sure Honey had done it a lot already. And more. The men would probably like that. Stupid little cunt.

Cunt.

That's the thing she has between her legs. I'm pretty sure of that. I know it's what Lizzie has. I've seen it. Like that time. After she yelled and went, rrrr rrrr rrrr, she passed out. With her skirt up to her waist. Or the time she came into Honey's room naked to get one of the men back out. Sometimes Lizzie falls down so I can see right up inside it.

Honey pretends not to look. Even though she plays with her own. At least with the one small part that sticks down.

And sometimes she asks the boys to touch her there. But she won't look. She's afraid to look. She's afraid to see what she looks like. Or what Lizzie does. Down there. What Lizzie uses to play with the men. What makes the boys want to play with her. I know exactly what it looks like. Exactly. But I won't tell. Except that Lizzie's is much bigger than hers. I'll tell you that.

Lizzie's not a little cunt. Lizzie's a big cunt. I wanted Honey to shout that. But it was too dangerous. That's what I mean about being a prisoner. Anything might happen then. Anyone who watches the movies knows that. You don't go up against the Warden. Not unless you have an escape plan. That's why it's good to stick with those boys. Our brave companions. And to never tell. She'd never get freed, no matter what she did.

Though I was mad then. After that happened. Really mad. But I don't know who I was mad at worse. Her for getting herself into that mess, or Lizzie, or the boys. But it did make me sick of waiting so much.

The next time they were playing, they played they were prisoners. I think they need to practice that too, especially Honey and her brother, to help make them tough for the long nights. Even if they don't know that prisoners is what they really are.

They were using the croquet mallets from the old croquet set to pretend they were convicts on the chain gang. They've never learned to play croquet. Not any of them. Knocking the wooden balls through the metal hoops. And now there's no grass left in the backyard to roll the balls over. And no balls either. They all got taken away when someone broke a window tossing one through the air. So they just hammer at the dirt. Wham, wham, wham, they hit the ground. Wham, wham, wham.

Until that one time her brother knelt down inside the pit they'd dug with their hammering, there weren't any rocks to bust, just lumps of dirt, and he wanted to see something. To check something out, he said.

He still says I tried to kill him.

No, that's not true. He thinks she did. And that's what he told Lizzie. Mom, he said, she tried to kill me. While Honey said she'd never do that. Shaking her head and sobbing. Not ever she said. He'd just knelt down like that, right when she was about to hammer. When she had the mallet all the way up in the air. And there was no way she could stop the blow from falling.

Lizzie just squeezed her lips together. And hugged the brother. And took him to the doctor to get stitches. That he could brag about for a long time. Touching the bald spot on his head where the doctor shaved.

To her, Lizzie just said, I don't know what to do with you. You're so violent. Other girls aren't like that. And Lizzie shook her head. You have to stop playing with boys. While Honey whimpered, just like all the other little girls. And said how sorry she was. And kept repeating: It was an accident. An accident.

While I just thought about how much I liked watching the blood pour down, all down his head and into his eyes. While he screamed and she apologized.

I don't mind the sight of blood. I don't think I ever have. Even when it's mine. Or hers. Ours. Like when she cut her hand wide open chasing her brother and his friend, to pour water on them. To water them like plants. When she tripped and fell on the glass she was carrying.

When she opened her hand wide to look you could see the joint of the middle finger. It was between white and transparent, like plastic. Cartilage, it's called. I think she fainted then. And left me to carry on. I ran water over the cut to clean it, and when the blood was washed away the inside looked like meat. I never knew we were meat before. Just like steak.

One of the men who sleeps with Lizzie eats raw steak when he has a hangover. It's funny with Lizzie though. She just drinks milk and treats everyone nice. Giving out hugs like free gifts at a bank opening. I'm the only one who can't stand it. I won't go near Lizzie then. Feel bad, act nice. It's strange. I like it better the other way: Act bad, feel nice. That's what I do.

Lizzie wasn't home when Honey cut her hand. She was out drinking. So no one ever took Honey out for stitches. Though Lizzie did scream at her later. When she was drunk. I don't think Lizzie called her a cunt that time. Or threatened to make her show off to the men the way she did to her brother's friends. Getting all undressed. Lizzie just told Honey how mean and stupid and clumsy she was.

I bet you can understand by now why Honey can't tell. About anything. Why she always has to be brave. And prove herself by letting them do those things to her.

Her brother helped her with her hand. And his friend. They helped put on the bandages, and squeezed her arm till it stopped bleeding. And were proud of how I didn't cry. But just did what had to be done. The way the men do in those war comics. Always helping their wounded buddies. Bandaging them while they bite bullets and snarl. They were brave companions then. Very brave. Just like me. When I wouldn't let Honey tell Lizzie why she had hit her brother over the head. I knew it was a trick. To find out more about those things she does. So I just sang my song.

Early on a Sunday morning
High up in a gallows tree
Kevin Barry gave his young life
For the cause of liberty

I think that's what they do to you when you kill someone. Or when you keep dangerous secrets. You have to give your life. The gallows is the place where they hang you. Or maybe they give you the chair. That's what her brother's friend says.

They give you the chair. I don't think that's in a tree though. Sometimes it's what they do when they tie Honey up. They give her the chair. That's what they did after she hit him like that. They said they would give her the chair for trying to kill him.

Honey just smiled her usual smile and I let them do it. While she licked her lips. And felt it down there again. Because she thought she deserved it. That punishment. Maybe that's how Lizzie feels when the men hit her. Maybe she thinks she deserves it. For getting out of line. Though I don't know why. Or which comes first. The feelings down there or the wanting to be punished.

When they had Honey all tied up, they got out some old wires and tied them around her. And told her they were going to plug her in. This is it, they kept saying. This is it. This is what happens to murderers. This is it. And they laughed while she screamed.

I didn't murder him, I didn't even try to murder him, she blubbered. It was an accident. While I just told her to shut up and be quiet. To learn to be brave. That she had to be prepared. For anything. After all, someday this might happen for real. She has to learn to take it.

I was scared. At least for a moment. I didn't expect the wires. They made me think the boys might actually do it. Though I didn't think anything would happen. I didn't think they had the wires in the right places. And they didn't attach one down there. Even if they said they would.

What I do when it's scary like that, even when it's Lizzie or the men threatening her, is I think how nice it would be not to have this body. How if I'm proud and brave like Kevin Barry, God My Father might give me another one. If I'm very brave, He should give me my choice. I should get whatever body I want.

Sometimes I spend a lot of time on that. Getting it perfect. I think I would start with her body. Build on that. I'd make the hair lighter and curly, so it wouldn't just hang down like a bowl, but shine around my head like a crown. Though I'd keep her eyes, and her teeth from before she broke them. And the hand from before it was cut.

She has problems opening her right hand sometimes now. The joint doesn't seem to work just the way it should anymore. But she's still strong. And she runs faster than anyone on the block. And she can climb. Even with the bad hand she can still grip. When that thing between her legs doesn't make her silly. And want to giggle or be punished.

So I'd leave that out. Definitely. And the breasts as well. The ones Lizzie says she should start growing any day now. To shove in the faces of the men, Lizzie says.

On the other hand, I don't think I'd give myself a prick either. That's what Lizzie calls what the brother has down there when she's been drinking. I don't think she really wants him to do what the men do to her with theirs. I think she just says that to him to make him feel ashamed and useless. The way she tells him how small it is. I don't think it's nearly that small. I've seen it. And I know he can do things with it. I've seen that too. It's just like calling Honey a useless little cunt.

Around here everyone gets to feel useless. Though it's easier on her brother because when Lizzie makes him feel useless him and his friend can make Honey feel useless. It's like a chain. A chain of command, like in the Army. Only it's a chain of uselessness. With the men at the top and Honey at the bottom.

There must be something that makes the men feel useless. I think that's why they cry sometimes when they drink. But I don't know what it is. I think about it sometimes as I wait. I don't feel useless. I know my turn will come. And I'm not going to screw someone like Lizzie. That's what she hollers sometimes when she brings a man home. Just before she starts to sing, rrrr rrrr rrrr. I'm going to do something else.

The boys do seem very proud of their penises though. And I know they wouldn't be so hard on Honey if she had one. Though they're hard on each other, too. Doing things so they can practice being brave. So that one can be bigger or tougher than the other. So they'll know how to hold up under torture. They even do things to each other with their penises. And to their penises. Like threaten to cut them off.

Penis is what Lizzie calls what the boys have down there when she's sober. I use it because it's probably more proper to say that when you ask God for a body. Like calling a cunt a vagina. The penises make the boys silly. Just the way Honey is when she gets that feeling down there. Or Lizzie. Or the men. They all get that same funny look in their eyes.

That's why I think I'd leave that area out all together. So I won't need any of those words, unless God My Father asks me to make a choice. I'd even erase the nipples. That get played with to help her breasts grow.

I'd make my new body smooth all over. Maybe I wouldn't even have to pee, or do number two. Or maybe I could just pee a little, right out my belly button. And have no holes down there at all, where anything could be stuck, the way the boys like to stick their penises, or the men, while Lizzie sings, rrrr rrrr rrrr. Then I would never feel funny down there.

I could give myself wings instead. Wings would make me much more powerful than even a penis could. I could help other prisoners. I would really be an angel then. The Angel Kevin. I could do whatever I wanted. It would be easy to get even.

The way I wanted to when they did that thing with the wires. Because I was much more angry than I was scared. I spit at them and told them I'd get them back. And cried those awful angry tears. Even if I liked the blood, I still wouldn't want to kill him. I didn't know how they could think that. I know who my brave companions are. I would never turn informer. Betray them. Or kill them. Not either one of them. Or hurt them too badly. Sometimes I just enjoy hurting them a little. The way they hurt Honey.

Most of the time I help them. Just the way they helped her. Even against other gangs of boys in the neighbourhood. They're not the ones I'm after. Not her brother or his friend. They're not the ones. We're on the same side. They should know that.

Honey and her brother even visit each other and make their plans late at night when Lizzie is drinking in the house with the men. I help them. Especially when we get scared and don't know what's going to happen to us, what they'll do to us or make us do. We sneak from room to room like POWs sneaking from their bunks to plan their escapes.

So that it doesn't matter if they get silly and dress up sometimes and play Lizzie and the men. And Honey really does stick her cunt in her brother's face. Or just play with it on his bed. Because they act so brave. It's not practice anymore the way it is when I let them tie her up. Or when they pretend to hunt with his bow and arrow. And shoot targets. And small animals.

Mostly her brother's friend does that. I don't. I hate to see the animals die. But I think I'll have to learn. That way I'll be able to do what's necessary when the time comes. The way I already know how to shoot the rifles. Even the heavy one with the big bullets, the thirty calibre. When I breathe so slowly, and compensate for her arm wobbling, timing my shot. Bang. To hit the target dead centre. I like that better because I don't have to watch the light go out of the animals' eyes. And I know that if I keep it up, I'll figure out how to release the prisoners. And how to get even.

I think about doing it to the men sometimes. As my cheek hugs the rifle stock. Especially the ones who look at Honey like that. Just the way they do at Lizzie. When they say how pretty and cute Honey is. And sometimes other things. That she smiles at. When they ask her to come over. And squeeze her legs. All the way up. That's when I think that maybe I could do it. It might even be easy. Easier than with a little animal. I'm not sure. But then I just think there'd be more. Lizzie seems to have an infinite supply. And everything would be the same. I'm pretty sure they're not the ones I want either. They hardly count. Except for their eyes.

The last time Lizzie called Honey a cunt, and told her how stupid and useless she was, I knew then what I had to do. I almost did it. Especially after Lizzie pissed in the middle of the kitchen floor and sat in the puddle. And expected Honey to clean it up. I wanted Lizzie to pass out in the puddle herself. So that I would have time to find a weapon and do it right there while she snored. With the drool coming out her mouth and all the pee on the floor.

Or maybe I'd like it better if Lizzie was awake enough to fight back. The way she is sometimes when she attacks one of the kids with a stick or a poker or a knife. Coming at us across the room while she sings that song, rrrr rrrr rrrr. When it would be easy to take it away and get Lizzie back. Fighting hand to hand the way Kevin Barry did with the British soldiers. I think I'd like that. Though I don't think I'd want to see the blood. Or her eyes. Maybe I could just sing my song so I wouldn't have to.

'Twas only a lad of eighteen summers
Yet there's no one can deny
As he walked to death that morning
Proudly held his head up high

It's hard to think I might have to wait until I'm eighteen. Or Honey is. I can't believe I haven't been around longer than that already. That I haven't been waiting forever. When I realize how old I am and I think about making it to eighteen, I sing the song all over again. All the way from top to bottom. Again and again.

And it makes me feel brave. Because like I said, I'm the one who waits. For the right moment. For the perfect opportunity. Only it's still hard to think of waiting that long. Or that it might be longer. And then to have to be hanged. To have to watch them hang her. Or give her the chair.

That's when I think maybe it's not worth it. That I should just do it now to get it over with. Only she wouldn't be hanged then. Just put away. One of the men told her they do that to violent children who act crazy, because she struggled and yelled and I bit him when he tried to touch her. That they put people like that away forever. That wouldn't seem fair. There would just be more prison guards for her to smile at. And I wouldn't even get a new body then at all. That's when I think maybe I shouldn't bother with it. That it's best to keep on doing what I'm doing now. Just waiting. And trying to make her tougher. Because she's going to need that. To help her learn to brave all the torture she's still got coming. To help her learn to be silent, and to be strong. To help her make her getaway. Maybe she'll even be strong enough to take the boys along. To make good their escape.

Then when she's eighteen instead of being hanged, she'll be free. And far away from here. And then, if I want, I'll hang myself. Give my life for the cause of liberty. And I'll be gone. Like Kevin Barry, bravely taking all those secrets with me. My true name, and theirs, and all those other things the Warden and the guards wished to know. So Honey will be alone and even she will never know who I am. And no one except God My Father will ever be able to find me. Or know. How she was held prisoner. Or what she had to do to escape.

Maybe I will get my new body then, anyway. For being especially brave. And waiting so long. And holding my temper so well. So I'll be able to help someone else, flying down shrieking like a dive-bomber, my wings folded in like a hawk. And maybe I'll get to do what I've always wanted. Maybe I'll get to kill one of the tormentors.

I just hope it isn't her.

That without me she doesn't start acting like Lizzie all the time. Yelling and drinking and threatening and making fun of people. Telling them how useless they are. While she does all those things with that silly cunt of hers.

ONCE UPON A TIME

[She wants you to know that this is not a fiction. Is not. Is not. This is a telling. A way to the telling. A way to be able to tell. Important: the way to be able to tell. She can tell because she can tell it this way. As if she were the author. Only the author. (That fiction.) As if she had authority. The authority of the telling. (That other fiction.) Something she can hide behind if she wishes. Or hide in. A maze. A labyrinth. Of images or pain. In which to play hide and seek. The way she always does. Through changing, changing. By moments mute, by moments screaming. Always soft coloured. Blurred. A Victorian garden. Or pastel drawings. With fiction the condition of the text. Of the telling. A condition of her life, of her living. Of being allowed, of allowing herself, to live. Or to play. At authoring. At fiction. That is sometimes real, and sometimes only means something. Because she lies sometimes, and sometimes lies are the clearest way to the truth, to the meaning of the telling. Because even when she lies the pain is real. And this time she wants you to know it. The way she wants you to know the details are real. And I will be her witness. Swearing to the truth of what she tells because no matter how she tells it what she tells me in my mind appears in detail in my body. In detail on my body. Some days is my body.]

There is a story someone tells. That Julio Cortázar wrote. It's a story I keep hearing. A lot, actually. Sometimes I think they tell it to me. Sometimes I think I just hear it. Over and over. That I listen for it. For that particular story. Among all the stories that they tell.

Once upon a time there was a rapist, this story begins.

Or maybe it's a bit different. Maybe it doesn't begin that way at all. And maybe it's about a rape-murderer. I do know it's a mysterious and magical story. At least that's what they say. Because Julio Cortázar is a very great writer.

The story tells about this man who rapes this girl by a road and then she dies. Rape is when a man puts his penis inside a woman even if she doesn't want him to. The story says this rape took place somewhere in France. And they say it really happened. Some of them are quite sure about that. That he raped her and then she died.

Only I don't know how it happened. If he kills her or if

he just hurts her
  [and hurts her
  and hurts her
  and hurts her]
    so bad that he doesn't know how bad and then
he leaves her there by herself and then she dies. Like that.

And then maybe the police find him and maybe they
know what he's done so maybe they execute him. Or maybe
it's not like that at all because maybe it takes a long long time
or he has an accident or something. But then he's dead too.

And he meets the same girl over there on the other side
of death and she forgives him, and she makes love to him.
That's when a man does the same thing to a woman with his
penis only she wants him to. Maybe she even asks him to.
Because the rapist needed her and he felt so sorry
  [so sorry
  so sorry
  so sorry]
    and she had beautiful hair and he reached out
his hand.

And everyone was happy ever after even if they weren't
alive.

I don't believe that story. I don't believe it at all. I don't think
it's a true story even if they all repeat it and Julio Cortázar
wrote it and they say he was such a great writer. I don't think
it would happen like that, not at all, not even after death. I'm
quite sure it wouldn't. That's something I'm really sure about.
I wouldn't forgive anything like that. It wouldn't even matter
to me if he reached out his hand. I wouldn't care.

And I certainly wouldn't forgive him before he died the
way some people say they would. If the police didn't catch
him and they didn't get to execute him I know I wouldn't do
that. The way this woman Carolyn says she did when something like that happened to her. When this rapist who had

raped a lot of women came and raped her. Only he didn't hurt her so bad she died, he just hurt her
    [and hurt her
    and hurt her
    and hurt her]
        while her four-year-old son stood outside the door screaming and crying because he didn't understand what was happening to Mommy and she had to tell him to go back to sleep. To lie down in his room and go back to sleep she had to tell him that just to save his life and he was only four years old and so sad and that's even younger than I've been all this time sitting on my stair listening. And the rapist cut Carolyn with a little knife little tiny cuts and she bled a lot and still she forgave him. Even if she didn't die she forgave him
    [forgave him
    forgave him]
        anyway and told her son he had to forgive the rapist, too. Even if they were both so sad for the longest time still they were alive to forgive him. And they could live happily even if it wasn't ever after. And that was that.

I know that story's true because Carolyn still cries when she tells it only she's not sad anymore because it makes her feel so good to know she didn't kill him, she didn't even try to kill him, she forgave him and she's sure that makes her a good person. And so is everyone else. Only I still don't think I would do it and it wouldn't matter if I died or I didn't or if he died either. Or even if they would tell me what a good person I was and give me great big hugs the way Carolyn gave her son great big hugs after the rapist went away and the police came. It wouldn't even matter if they asked me to come down from my stair and gave me ice cream.

    Not if he got up on top of me and he grabbed my shoulders and he held me still and I couldn't move and I could hardly breathe and then he grabbed my chest and it didn't matter if I wasn't a woman at all because I had no breasts and what he pulled at was handfuls of skin or if he stuck his penis in from behind and it hurt

[and it hurt and it hurt

and it hurt and it hurt

and it hurt and it hurt

and it hurt and it hurt

and it hurt and it hurt

and it hurt and it hurt

and it hurt and it hurt]

and that's all I can tell you about it: It hurt so bad with him holding on and pushing in and grabbing at me with his hands digging into my shoulders and pulling at the skin on my chest while it hurt

[and it hurt and it hurt

and it hurt and it hurt

and it hurt and it hurt

and it hurt and it hurt]

just like that one two three four one two three four in and out and it hurt

[and it hurt

and it hurt

and it hurt

and it hurt

and it hurt]

so bad that I sometimes get stuck in it and I can't hardly stop saying it. Telling how it hurt

[and it hurt and it hurt

and it hurt and it hurt

and it hurt and it hurt

and it hurt and it hurt

and it hurt and it hurt]

and the pain was all yellow and blue and red mostly red hitting me and hitting me like the waves at the

shore hitting me and hitting me until I can't feel anything else
but how it hurt

    [and it hurt

    and it hurt

    and it hurt

    and it hurt

    and it hurt

    and it hurt

    and it hurt]

        until I'm all lost in how it hurt

    [and it hurt and it hurt

    and it hurt and it hurt

    and it hurt and it hurt

    and it hurt and it hurt

    and it hurt and it hurt

    and it hurt and it hurt

    and it hurt and it hurt

    and it hurt and it hurt]

        and there is nothing else but how it hurt

    [and it hurt and it hurt

    and it hurt and it hurt

    and it hurt and it hurt

    and it hurt and it hurt]

        and I don't know if I'm alive or if I'm dead
because it hurts

    [and it hurts and it hurts

    and it hurts and it hurts

    and it hurts and it hurts

    and it hurts and it hurts

    and it hurts and it hurts]

        until it doesn't matter anyway. Any of it.

I'm walking in a grey place and there's nothing there except
the pain and it won't go away and I'm lost and everything
hurts and I don't know where to go because it hurts

[and it hurts
    and it hurts
    and it hurts
    and it hurts
    and it hurts]
        the sky hurts and the ground hurts and the air
hurts and I don't care it doesn't matter at all because even if
it hurts and he grabs onto my shoulders and pulls at my chest:
still, I won't forgive him.
        Even if I'm lost and I can't find my stair where I like
to sit and play with my dolls and my little toy tea set stamped
made in China on the bottom of every cup while I listen to
their stories, there's still a little light that I can always find.
And it's sort of like a firefly and sort of like Tinkerbell in
Peter Pan. That's a book that I read sometimes too when I sit
on my stair, especially if their stories aren't very interesting.
        Only this is the light that reminds me that I won't
forgive him no matter what. No matter if I hurt and I'm lost
still I won't forgive him not even if I'm dead and I can't ever
come back not even as far as my stair still I will hold onto that
one light and I won't forgive him. Not ever.
        No matter if I float away the way she did in that
story soft hair billowing out all around her like in an ad for
Breck shampoo, the ones I used to see on the TV. While
I look down on him the way she did on that rapist so far away
and sorry. Still I won't forgive him no matter how far away
I get or how long I wait or how beautifully my hair billows
out. Or even if I'm very close and he reaches out his hand and
calls my name.
    And says please
    [please
    please
    please
    please
    please]

and touches my hair, I did have beautiful hair, still it wouldn't matter. Even if the hurting seemed to stop it wouldn't matter. Because no matter how much it seemed to stop hurting it would still hurt. Deep inside it would still hurt
       [and hurt
       and hurt
       and hurt
       and hurt
       and hurt]
       and I still wouldn't know how to find my way back and I wouldn't know who I was except that I am the one who won't forgive him.
       Even if he said I'm sorry
       [I'm sorry
       I'm sorry
       I'm sorry]
       still I wouldn't forgive him. No matter how long he kept saying I'm sorry
       [I'm sorry I'm sorry
       I'm sorry I'm sorry
       I'm sorry I'm sorry
       I'm sorry I'm sorry]
       how could I do this to you I'm sorry
       [I'm sorry
       I'm sorry
       I'm sorry]
       and he reached out his hand and he wiped off my tears and he said it again I'm sorry
       [I'm sorry
       I'm sorry
       I'm sorry
       I'm sorry]
       it wouldn't matter at all. No matter what I said right then it wouldn't matter at all. Even if I let him bathe me and he was so gentle and he smiled his gentlest smile and he

wiped away my tears still it wouldn't matter at all. Not even after he went away and he got married and he smiled at that girl just like that his gentlest smile, the one he had always saved for me, as I looked at him lift the veil she wore, so much like one of my dolls. Whether I could already see from the way she looked at him how easily she would forgive him all the things I knew he was going to do, even then it wouldn't matter. Even if he died after a terrible accident it wouldn't matter. It wouldn't matter at all.

    Because even if he kept saying I'm sorry

      [I'm sorry

      I'm sorry]

        how could I do this to you you're so beautiful

    [so beautiful

    so beautiful]

        you're so beautiful and good, one two three four in and out

      [in and out in and out

      in and out in and out

      in and out in and out

      in and out in and out

      in and out in and out

      in and out in and out]

        you're so beautiful and good how could I do this to you

    [this to you

    this to you]

        how could I do this to anything so beautiful and good

    [and good and good

    and good and good

    and good and good

    and good and good

    and good and good

    and good and good]

         while he went in and out
     [in and out in and out
     in and out in and out
     in and out in and out
     in and out in and out]
        it wouldn't matter.
Even if he bathed me and I didn't bite his hand and he washed away my tears and I still didn't bite his hand it wouldn't matter. Whether he promised me he would always love me and he would come back and he would marry me and not that girl, he would never marry her, because he was so sorry that he would do anything if I forgave him. Anything at all if I would just forgive him.

    Still I wouldn't forgive him no matter what I said I wouldn't forgive him
     [forgive him
     forgive him
     forgive him
     forgive him]
       even if I said I forgave him
     [forgave him
     forgave him
     forgave him
     forgave him
     forgave him]
       even if I said I had forgiven him
     [forgiven him
     forgiven him
     forgiven him
     forgiven him
     forgiven him]
       even if I said I would forgive him
     [forgive him
     forgive him
     forgive him]

even if I said I was all right
[all right
all right
all right
all right
all right]
even if I said it was all right
[all right all right
all right all right
all right all right
all right all right]
even if I said I loved him too
[loved him too
loved him too]
and that he could do it again
[again again
again again
again again
again again
again again]
push in and out
[in and out
in and out
in and out
in and out
in and out
in and out]
again
[again
again
again]
as much as he liked. If he really wanted to. And
if he would reach out and touch my hair.

That's a lie. What I said was a lie. It's not nearly even as true as Julio Cortázar. That's right: I was lying. Even if I said all that right then I was lying. Because I know that if he died and I died and it was after death and we were right there together like those two people in that story and he reached out for me and he touched my hair I wouldn't forgive him. I would never let him do anything like that to me. Not ever again.

Because I could go away. And it wouldn't even matter if it was into that field of pain because I wouldn't have to listen to him. And I would never invite him to make love to me
   [love to me
   love to me]
      no matter what I wouldn't even if I had breasts like that other girl he married and he could touch my hair. And it wouldn't even matter that they say I'm just a little girl who has never grown up because I know now that I don't have to say those things. And I especially wouldn't have to say all those things if I were already dead and there was nothing he could take away from me. Not ice cream. Or big hugs. And it's been so long since anybody touched my hair.

So I just know I wouldn't say anything like that. I wouldn't at all. I'll just turn to him from my stair and nya nya nyanyanya I'll say I'll never forgive you. Even if all those other people forgive you
   [forgive you
   forgive you
   forgive you
   forgive you]
      I'll never forgive you.
   [never forgive you
   never forgive you
   never forgive you
   never forgive you]

Even if the whole world forgives you I still
won't. Not ever.
    [not ever not ever
    not ever not ever
    not ever not ever
    not ever not ever]
       Not ever no matter what even if I'm the only one
who won't do it
    [won't do it
    won't do it]
      I won't do it.
    [won't do it won't do it
    won't do it won't do it
    won't do it won't do it
    won't do it won't do it]
      I won't do it.
    Because you can stay in hell forever for all I care. Just stay
there. That's right: Stay there. Because no one should ever
hold anyone by the shoulders and the skin on the chest while
he pushes
    [and pushes
    and pushes
    and pushes
    and pushes
    and pushes]
      in and out
    [in and out
    in and out
    in and out
    in and out
    in and out]
      so that it hurts
    [and it hurts and it hurts and it hurts
    and it hurts and it hurts and it hurts

and it hurts and it hurts and it hurts
and it hurts and it hurts and it hurts
and it hurts and it hurts and it hurts
and it hurts and it hurts and it hurts]

and they have to go away and they don't know if they're dead or they're alive or even where they are and they have to walk through a grey field where they can't see anything and everything hurts. And it never stops hurting. And they get so sad that they die they just die.

So that's what I'm going to tell you: You can just stay in hell as far as I'm concerned. Even if you're not dead you can stay in hell because I won't forgive you. I never forgave you no matter how many times you said you were sorry or you wiped away my tears still I never forgave you and you deserve to be in hell and that's that. Because I didn't deserve to hurt like that even if you washed me and said you were sorry I didn't deserve to hurt like that.

And I certainly didn't want to be so sad that I died.

No. I don't want to be so sad that I'll die forever while it hurts

[and it hurts and it hurts
and it hurts and it hurts
and it hurts and it hurts
and it hurts and it hurts
and it hurts and it hurts
and it hurts and it hurts]

and I'll never be happy like Sleeping Beauty or Cinderella or Snow White or even Carolyn and her son who got lots of ice cream. While all I'll get to do is listen to them talk about that woman who forgave that man when he reached out his hand. And I don't want to listen to that anymore, certainly not for forty more years, you can just bet on that, I've made up my mind what to say.

To that rapist and to Julio Cortázar and to that hand

reaching out and to that hand washing all the tears off that
face and to that man holding onto those shoulders. Go to hell
I say go to hell.

   [go to hell go to hell
   go to hell go to hell
   go to hell go to hell
   go to hell go to hell
   go to hell go to hell]
    Go to hell.

  Only it doesn't matter what I say. They never listen to
what I say when they tell those stories they just tell me to go
away. Go away

   [go away
   go away
   go away
   go away
   go away]

   they say. Nothing ever happened to you they say
what can you tell us about it they say you're always making
up stories. How would you know

   [would you know
   would you know
   would you know]

   what to do how would you know

   [would you know
   would you know
   would you know]

   anything about it you're just a little girl who's
never grown up you just keep saying the same thing over and
over,

   [over and over
   over and over
   over and over]

   you always repeat yourself you're not even

interesting, you've never been to any place like that where it
hurt

    [and it hurt and it hurt
    and it hurt and it hurt
    and it hurt and it hurt
    and it hurt and it hurt
    and it hurt and it hurt]

      so why don't you just play with your dolls, you
know that you don't know anything about it. And besides
that, you're not like Julio Cortázar, you're not a great writer.

And that's when I think about how to fool them. They
think I'm still listening to them but I'm hardly listening at all.
I have other games besides my dolls and my tea set, I've
learned a lot from all those books he left me, that's why I'm
sure I can figure out how to do it. And it won't make any difference how long I've sat here or how often I repeat myself
because even if I've waited for so many years and even if they
don't think they want to listen still I'm going to tell them. I'm
going to find a way to trick them into listening to me.

Then pretty soon they'll want to hear how it hurt

    [and it hurt and it hurt
    and it hurt and it hurt
    and it hurt and it hurt
    and it hurt and it hurt]

      Because I'm going to walk back into that grey
place where everything is the same and I'm going to make it
different. Each pain will have its colour and I won't get lost
in the blue and the red and the yellow and the pounding
waves I'm going to learn the difference between all the possible colours and all the patterns I'm going to learn all about
them. About red and yellow and blue and pain

    [and pain and pain and pain
    and pain and pain and pain
    and pain and pain and pain

and pain and pain and pain
and pain and pain and pain
and pain and pain and pain]
      until I won't have to repeat myself at all. Because it won't be all the same any more it will be all different. A beautiful marvellous magical different field of hurt and mountain of ache and ocean of searing and earth of bruising
[of bruising
of bruising
of bruising]
      and cave of cutting
[of cutting
of cutting]
      and I'll be the Pied Piper.

That's another favourite story I read over and over, only I won't have a flute, I'll invite them all in with my words. My red and blue and green and magical mysterious words. I'll lure them into my cave where it hurts
[and it hurts and it hurts
and it hurts and it hurts
and it hurts and it hurts
and it hurts and it hurts
and it hurts and it hurts
and it hurts and it hurts
and it hurts and it hurts]
      and I won't let them out again.

Until they listen for the longest time and they tell me they believe me and that my story is just as magical and just as mysterious and just as beautiful as Julio Cortázar even if it only begins: Once Upon a Time There Was a Little Girl. A little girl so little that she believed everything she was told.

Even when he said how sorry he was and how he would never do it again. And he reached out and he touched her hair. And told her how he loved her and how she was beautiful

and how he was sorry and how she should forgive him. And
how he would come back to marry her when she grew up.

Then, after they listen, they'll ask me what I would do and I'll
tell them. About how you never forgive people who hurt you.
        [and hurt you and hurt you
        and hurt you and hurt you
        and hurt you and hurt you
        and hurt you and hurt you
        and hurt you and hurt you
        and hurt you and hurt you]
        You send them to hell and that's that.
    And they'll all nod and say how true that is, how true my
story is, even that woman Carolyn will say that, how it's so
much truer than Julio Cortázar. And then I'll let them out for
ice cream and it won't matter at all if nothing like that ever
happened to me. If no one ever held me down and grabbed
my shoulders and the skin on my chest and forced his penis
into me. And it never hurt.
        [never hurt
        never hurt
        never hurt]
        No, it never did. And no one told me that I was
good and I was beautiful and that he loved me and he didn't
understand how he could do this to me he was so sorry.
        [so sorry
        so sorry]
    And I was never so sad that I died.
    I've just been here listening all along. And playing with
my dolls and sipping tea out of my little china tea set with my
pinky finger raised while I look at those books that he gave
me with all their pretty pictures while I sit on my stair right
above his door just where I've been ever since he went away
waiting for him to come back just the way he said he would

because nothing like that happened to me nothing at all not
ever even if I'll never forgive him and it hurt so much
　　[so much
　　　so much]
　　　　　he deserves to go to hell, you understand?

ATHENA, HONEY

I know something you don't know. I know something you don't know. I know something you don't know. That's what I keep saying. Again and again inside his head, that one who says he's going to kill me. It's what makes him so angry, sitting there, his head in his hands. What makes him hold onto himself, and shake back and forth. Until I can almost hear him say it, shout it, spit it out from between our teeth, I'll kill you, I'll kill you, just you wait, I'll kill you. But then he's been saying that for years.

So that I just laugh and dance, or I jump up and down as if I were skipping rope, or bouncing a ball to the sound of my chant, playing my girl games. Or even, when he's really mad and his hands come away from his head and clench themselves into fists and he pounds them on the pavement, or on the armrests of the chair where we sit, I turn and run, laughing, you can't get me you can't get me you'll never get me, repeating it over and over. You can't get me you can't get me,

I know something you don't know until he starts to shake our head back and forth farther and farther shoulder to shoulder or bangs it against a wall, thinking maybe that way he'll shake me loose or find me, that he'll be able to do it, that thing he once thought he could. Those days he still thought he only spared me out of kindness, way back then. When he thought my secret would be the easiest thing in the world to find out. Or that he already knew it, and I just thought he didn't.

Because it's not the fact that he's a she, he knows that already, after all, all he has to do is look down there between his legs, and besides, he looks down so often. Only it's usually at the sidewalk. Out in the world where he works so much, gets so much done, moving and shaking, he calls it. But always, the eyes trying to fix themselves, just in front of that spot in his blue jeans, or his slacks, where it ought to be, that thing he ought to have, only he never does — look I mean. Even if his eyes sometimes run over the cloth of the pants, over and over, the way his tongue does over his teeth or the inside of his mouth, until he notices it and then the tongue shrinks away to rest in the middle, our mouth hollow around it, and his eyes look far away. He doesn't want to remember his body, even the wetness of our mouth, feel it from the inside, he never has. Though he's sure it would be worse to have a body if you had to admit to having what I have, that would be the worst of all, to have to feel that, to know he has yet another entrance into his body, besides his mouth, or his ass hole. I like to say it like that. Two words. Ass hole. It makes it a real place, and that makes him angry, too.

He only likes it as something he can call people: Asshole asshole asshole, real quick. The way he calls them big shit full of shit, and says piss on you and shitface asshole and won't think about how food goes in and shit and pee come out. He doesn't like it how I might smear it around the walls, the way I maybe once did our room, I might like to do that still, to do

189

that and to tell him about all those other things he hates, he's such a bore, thinking he's an action figure.

The kind they sell in stores, like Batman or Superman or Luke Skywalker, every year there are more and he just adds them on, a piece here and a piece there, more and more of those plastic things without bodies. Bigger, better, more the way each year he can do more, more work more talk more action, more smiles more frowns more people to listen. While he won't admit that he's any more than plastic fists or fingers or feet.

Or talk. Words. Hundreds of words. Rearranged in different poses, like the action figures. New and different but somehow always the same. All deployed around a hollow place. He just wraps our whole body in action figure plastic and words, and won't feel it, even when he looks down at his breasts. And he won't let me feel it either, except that I do sometimes. Which is when he screams at me about how he's going to kill me, because my feelings always come out of right down there, there in that one place he hates the most, and he won't even understand when I tell him how much fun it is. To feel that way.

He has terrible dreams, ones I'm in too, so that sometimes he sees me then, that's when he chases me, as I run from him, I know something you don't know I know something you don't know I know something you don't know. Only when he threatens to kill me, I'll kill you I'll kill you he shouts or screams or whispers between clenched teeth, tossing and turning in the bed, sweating and hitting out, sometimes he really thinks he kills someone, there in the dream.

But it's never me. Not me. And not her either, our mother, the one he calls Lizzie, that one who caused all this, the other one he still threatens, at least in his mind, she was once the only one he threatened to kill, her and all those men. Me, he just threatened to beat up, I'll beat you if you keep acting like her, he'd say. Beat me, or tie me up.

Now it's me he threatens all the time. Because I laugh at him, the way she always did, drinking and singing, and telling him how useless he was, how he'd never amount to anything. And because I make him feel things down there. While I sing too. Only it's not rrrr rrrr rrrr, the way Lizzie once did, it's I know something you don't know, while there he is stuck looking at them, at the bodies.

And they're not like action figures either, like pulling apart one of those plastic dolls he still buys for himself in toy shops, whatever the newest ones are, from the newest movies, that he then gives away to the children. The dream people aren't like that at all, they're real bodies, as close as he's ever come to real bodies. Except for seeing the bodies of animals or birds dead on the road, or sides of beef in butcher shops or rabbits that he might skin himself, though he doesn't do that so much any more, first pulling off the fur, a long rip back toward himself with his hand, then taking out the entrails, making those animals all bloody and fragmented and horrible, because even if they are all muscle like the figures he likes they're still not plastic. With the bodies in the dreams like that too, or like the bodies in those horror movies he watches, replaying the parts where there is always somebody screaming. There are no words at all when they scream. He just watches.

And licks his lips, thinking of doing that, of making someone scream and scream, all hard and cold and shaking and sweating, while I'm the one who feels it down there, I'm the one who remembers how nice it is to scream and scream until someone comforts you, the way I sometimes scream and scream at him, longing for that moment, postponing that moment, that I am sure will feel so good, so very good, the way it always does. So that even if it doesn't happen, at all or for a long time, but the torment goes on and on until you have to go somewhere else because you hurt so much, still you'll always know it's there, that moment, and how good it can feel, that comfort that's coming, no matter what, you make sure you believe that it's no matter what. So that imagining that moment, from wherever you are, even if it's very far away, will always get you through the last little moment before it all changes, before they tell you how good you are, how very good and precious, those people who watch you who touch you who look at you, who do things to you as you beg.

While he just looks at those movies. And then when he starts to feel what I feel, right down there, even if it's because he wants to beat instead of beg, he still doesn't like it anymore, and he shuts off the TV and he starts to get sick. With that funny sick feeling he can get sometimes, that makes him run to the john right after he skins the rabbit or even when he remembers as he eats it. So that he has to go do that thing he won't admit to, the horror coming all squishy from his bowels.

Which makes him think that's the secret. That's what I know that he doesn't. Something he feels so vaguely somewhere inside him, that he's sure I remember how nice that can be, the screaming and screaming. While maybe I might imagine being skinned like that, oh yes, yes, I might say, begging them to hurt me more, just a little more, so that maybe that's why he imagines it, how that's what he'll do to me, maybe it's that he loves me, the way they always loved me, so I tell him that, you still love me, I say, you still love me, you still love me, you promised to protect me, you still love me.

Until that's a chant, too, you still love me you still love me, see how much, you still love me. While he screams as loud as he can, madder than ever, his voice hoarse with frustration, that he never did he never did HE NEVER DID, he was just doing his duty, he was doing what he was supposed to do.

But I could never learn he couldn't teach me anything how could you love somebody who couldn't learn anything, while now he's going to teach me for sure, this time for sure he's going to teach me to stop laughing at him. To stop making fun. So that he just explodes the way he used to when he beat up the boys, and suddenly there they are. All those bodies without their heads without their limbs without their guts. While all he has is his limbs. His hands his fingers his feet his words. That's all.

Only when he looks for me there among all those bloody torsos, their limbs cut off and flying about, or heaped up in piles, trying to see me among all those dismembered bodies, those talking heads, sometimes he screams that too, I'll dismember you, I'll dismember you, I'll tear you limb from limb, he can never find me. Even if those heads try to tell him things, whisper strange secret things in babbling voices he can never quite understand, that are almost but never quite I know something you don't know I know something you don't know. Because those heads are never quite me, I'm never quite there, I'm already somewhere else and they all look just a little more like him with his short hair and dirty bruised cheeks and frown.

As they tell him how the one who did this to them, committed all these terrible acts, already got away, she got away he got away they got away, a long time ago, a long long time ago, as the voices the heads, even the torsos, their chests moving in and out, laugh and laugh, the way I laugh and laugh, far away and in the distance until he hears my voice again, hears it clearly. Which tells him he must go after that person again, whoever it is that did this, so that he never remembers that it's him, that he did it, trying to find me, trying to find the secret that haunts him, he doesn't even know why those bodies those heads those limbs those toes those fingers are there, so that now he believes that someone tried to get him, that some evil stalks him, until when he hears my voice again, far away and calling, he's sure it's me, that this is what I've done, calling out, I know something you don't know, I know something you don't know, I know something you don't know.

That's why he never remembers how he's done it. Even if he does it again and again. Shouting I'll kill you I'll kill you, I'll dismember you, I'll tear you limb from limb, as he starts off again. Only he isn't sitting now, not really and not in the dream. In one place he's curled up into a ball his fingers in my mouth, in the other he's running, running, still screaming about how he'll wring my neck like a chicken. As if he hadn't just tried that. And wound up dismembering all those people who look just like him, when I'd only just raised my skirt up a bit so that he could see exactly what he has down there, under his pants, as if that were the secret anyway.

But maybe it does bring him closer to remembering, all that running and threatening and dismembering bringing him just that little bit closer the way the screams do, maybe it's a little reminder of what secret it is I do know. Maybe that's why he never wants to look down there, never look down there at all, believe he has one of those, maybe that's it. That what he would see between his legs, or mine, if he looked would be a so much bigger hint about this secret that's a so much bigger secret than just how he pees and shits, how peeing and shitting aren't just names you call someone, pisshead asshole shitface. My secret's a lot bigger than that no matter how many times he says those words or how much those things disgust him, how much he just tries to ignore them, even sitting on the toilet, humming or reading while he pretends there's nothing coming out of his body, all warm and sweet and sticky smelly at once.

Something he'll never want to smell because it's too much like when Lizzie would pee in her bed or some of the men, maybe they might pee on her, or on me, and there would be her breath after she would drink and drink. Whiskey they call that other stuff they would give me, the stuff that burns when you swallow it, just like the pee, some-times if I whimpered just a little too much they would make me do that. When they told me what a good dirty little girl I was how good I was but how much dirtier I was, so very very dirty with how much I liked those things they did with me down there, how much I really did, see, didn't I didn't I. And they would make me drink just a little to prove it, a little bit of pee, and more of the whiskey, pouring out the sides of my mouth, because it was hard to swallow and it hurt going down. When they would laugh again and feel me again and tell me how much I liked it, as much as my mother did, the drink or those feelings, those wonderful dirty feelings, didn't I didn't I didn't I.

And then they would do those other things that felt good and then they didn't and then I would scream and then I would ask them to stop, and then I wouldn't know where I was anymore it was just someone somewhere screaming and asking them to stop begging them to stop while I tried to find a place where I was me and I could hold on to that one last moment that I was sure would be there at the end, the moment of them stopping. And once more feeling my face and laughing and telling me how very good I was, how much they loved me when I was so very good like that. While I would always hold on to that one moment because I knew it would come soon it would, no matter how they tore at me, with their hands their mouths those other parts of their bodies, the parts like he wants to have, rubbing and laughing and spitting and dripping until I didn't know who I was except that in the end even if I had all that stuff all over my face they would still rub their hands on my face and comfort me. So that I didn't even need him then. To tell me he loved me that way he used to even if he denies it now, while instead he tells me that he'll kill me. Because he doesn't want to remember.

To know how much fun it was. To cry and cry and cry like that and have those hands all over your body, comforting you. He couldn't know, he doesn't want to know, how good it felt, to be loved so much they couldn't help it, that's what they always said, that they couldn't help it, they just couldn't help it, that's what they always said, they just couldn't help it. What they still say, hurting me and repeating themselves, how dirty and good and good and dirty I am, making me cry and beg. Just as they cried and begged, they did you see they did, they do you see they do, while he doesn't want to understand that, not at all. Which is why I try to explain it to him. How much I could like it, how much Lizzie could like it. How much I still do. That that's why she made me do all those things. She didn't hate me the way he says she hated us. She just knew I would like it.

And raising my skirt up like that, I try to tell him. How much fun that little thing between your legs can be, sweet little cunt, they always called it, and laughed, the way Lizzie did, only she called it a dirty little cunt, just the way she did me. And she wasn't really punishing me at all by letting them do that to me because she knew that when they comforted me it would be better than all her hugs put together. Just the way it can be when someone comes and puts that little part of you in their mouth and tells you how sweet you are how sweet your little cunt is. So that it feels so good even if you have to drink just a little bit of pee, or something like that anyway, that's really all right. So that sometimes I play with it down there, rubbing it between my fingers, and I say that, sweet little cunt, dirty little cunt, just to show him. Because he doesn't really know about that. I'm not even sure he was there. At least not all the time.

Which is why I chant. Because all that good feeling isn't really the secret, even if he thinks it is, if he thinks he just wants to kill me because I know how much fun that is, and he doesn't, he thinks it's hateful, horrible, still that's not my secret. We all know that.

And he must, too, since he screams and yells and clenches his fists and says he's going to kill me because I'm lying, liar liar pants on fire, things like that can't ever be fun. Not ever.

And he'll skin me like a rabbit just for saying different. Being dirty and bad and enjoying that so much, those things, that thing between your legs. That he tries to convince me could never be any fun at all, not when they touch you and play with you and do whatever they want not ever, it couldn't ever be any fun at all, any more than having those feelings between your legs could, no matter what you have down there. Until he doesn't even ever want to cry, he says it's because he's big and brave, but I know it's because he never wants anyone to hug him. Or to comfort him. Not even me. Because then he might believe that he's the one who's done something bad.

Which is another reason he might think I sit around and call it out, I know something you don't know, I know something you don't know, I know something you don't know. That I know he's really pretending, pretending really hard, so that no one will ever know how afraid he is that if someone hugs him maybe he'll find out he likes it. Or if someone touches him there, in that there he pretends he doesn't have, how he might like that. Which is why I ask him if he wants me to do it, to touch him, to hug him, to do it *right* there, just where I like it, where Lizzie likes it, where all those men like it. The way they taught me to do. And then when he screams and yells and threatens, when I run away again, I rub myself there as I'm singing, na-na-na boo-boo you can't get me you can't get me, I say, holding it in my hands, that thing between my legs.

I don't think I'll ever tell him what the secret really is. No matter what he does. Even if he grabs me and chokes me like one of those heads, the times I do get too close, if he tries to wring my neck like a chicken, the way he threatens, it still won't matter. Even as he shouts, I'll kill you, I'll kill you, I'll choke you till you tell me, I'll burn your feet, I'll pull out your fingernails, as he grabs a pair of bleeding legs, or arms, or another head, even if he does say things like that, I don't think I'll ever have to tell him. My head will just continue to speak there between his hands saying, if you kill me you'll never know will you, will you? And I'll cackle like a witch, will you will you, will you, laughing just the way Lizzie once did, as he gets wilder and chokes me more. And maybe I'll tell him just a little, give him a little tidbit, or little tidbits, until he screams and lets go. I don't think it will take too much to make him scream and let go, not when he starts to see where I'm going, with the blood all over his dream hands, as I start, with just the beginning of it.

That I know where he comes from. Not where babies come from but where he comes from. That's all it would take, just the littlest hint, and I'd be free again, running and running, na-na-na boo-boo, you can't get me. While he would follow shouting, I'll kill you I'll kill you I'll skin you alive. As I just giggle. Giggle and run, run and giggle, chanting and shouting, maybe I'll even stop long enough to lift up my skirt, to ask him if he'll do that, please, will he, will he, do what they would, to make me beg. And I'll lick my lips as he just gets madder and madder, while I chant it again, I know something you don't know I know something you don't know, I know something you don't know, savouring each word between my teeth, better than pee, or whiskey, or any of that other stuff, that got smeared on my face. Or that I think did.

So I think about how I'll never tell him. It makes me feel so good, to know that one thing he'll never know. That he'll never have any reason to know. That I'll protect him from, no matter how much I tease him. Because if he knew, it's not me he'd dismember. I know that even if he doesn't. It's himself he'd kill. This time on purpose. Tear himself limb from limb, and then choke himself till his tongue stuck out, all blue, the way he almost does, almost knowing it, again and again. He'd just pick up one of those heads, the way he always does, but this time he would choke it and choke it, and it wouldn't be me and it wouldn't be her, it would be himself with his sullen face and his short hair, the way it always is, only this time he would know it as he would choke it and choke it and choke it, that head, until he was dead. Maybe until we were dead, all of us.

He talks about it. Says he's like Athena, the goddess of wisdom, the one he reads about in school, that he makes into another action figure in his head, just like Wonder Woman. Who he insists he likes because she wasn't really a woman at all, that's why she was a wonder, she just looked like a woman, the way he does, and not too much, certainly not all flab and hanging things, the way he always says Lizzie looked sprawled on the bed with her white garter belt still on, her breath bubbling through her mouth. Not like that, Wonder Woman's not like that at all, and Athena isn't either, she's a goddess, born right out of the head of Zeus, her father, already wise and strong and good. And fierce, she's the goddess of war, too, always ready to do battle, to stand up for herself, just the way he says he is. Before he laughs and tells me how I should call him that now, it's a better name for him than Kevin, maybe he'll even be a woman and wear a dress if he can be a woman like that, and he deserves to be, he really does, because he was born that exact same way. Right out of the head of our father. He's sure of it. Even if he doesn't remember him, has no real idea what our father was like or if we really had a father at all, a real father, one he could find if he looked, who might hug us, the way our Mommy who isn't Lizzie did.

Then he tells me our father bore him right out of his head just to make sure I would be okay when our father went away, that he was born to protect me from evil. He was supposed to be a real superhero, a real one. Or even a goddess. Yes. That's what he was meant to be. So that it's too bad our father wasn't smarter and didn't know I was already just like Lizzie and not hardly worth protecting at all I'm so bad, most of the time I'm so bad, hardly someone a goddess, a superhero should be forced to spend so much time with, but still: That's the real story. He won't believe that our father went away long before he came along, he still says he was born that way, right from our father's head, he is sure of it.

Only I know something you don't know, I know something you don't know, I know something you don't know. And even if I'll never tell him I'll still always shout that at him because I like knowing I know and he doesn't, I like savouring it on my lips, especially when he acts so superior, saying those things about our father, and how I'm bad and he's good, so that I start to say it over and over. Oh, yeah, I say, well, I say, I know something you don't know, I know something you'll never know.

Because he's right. He wasn't born the normal way at all. And he was born to protect me, he's even right about that. Though it doesn't make him any better than I am, because, believe me, whether he wants it for his new name or not, he's no Athena either. Even if he didn't come slipping out of that hole, like a rabbit out of a hat. He wasn't all pink and squawling, even if his face was twisted up, when he was born. He was born full-blown all right, but it was hardly from our father's head, it was just that same place. That same place as ever.

Only it was different.

Very different. Very very different.

So very different that I don't think I've been sure of anything, anything at all, in the world or in my dreams, ever since. Except this. This one thing. That it happened this way. Just exactly this way. That time Lizzie was there. That one particular time. When he wasn't. Not even outside the door. When all those things happened. Those things that happened over and over and maybe started then or maybe didn't, but those things that were always possible when Lizzie looked like that her face all loose and distorted, her voice all slurred.

When the men were there or maybe they weren't and I was so scared always so scared always so very scared no matter how much I told myself it was fun it would be fun still it wasn't not really even if it felt good in that one place and I knew that they would be nice in the end I told myself that they would be nice in the end that she would be nice in the end that even if she wasn't nice she would go to sleep and wake up nice if only I kept going and kept still and I was good exactly the way they told me to be good in exactly the way they wanted me to be good and I did exactly what they wanted exactly what she wanted exactly what she told me to do when she called me names and told me how bad how dirty I was what a dirty little cunt I was or maybe that was later and this was the first time, maybe this was the first time she insulted me like that, and told me how bad I was, and maybe none of the men were there at all or maybe they were and maybe she was lying on the bed snoring or maybe she was laughing and maybe she grabbed me or maybe one of them did it's so hard to tell except that the room was all yellow and warm from the fire and she was naked and it smelled of drink and of medicine and they called me downstairs or maybe she did or maybe I was there already I think I was there already and she crossed the room in her white garter belt laughing. Laughing and laughing.

She laughed at me that dreadful laugh that she only ever had when she was like that and she smelled of whiskey while she did her little dance staggering around the room with the bottle in her hand and it was all so clear, so very very clear as that part of her body came closer and closer, closer and closer, that one part of her body below the white of the garter belt closer and closer until it was so close, all red brown and wrinkled and so very very close, so very very big and so very very close, that it still takes up my whole mind my whole vision paints itself on walls as I whimper in my throat and forget how to speak even to chant because I would rather be the only one who knows it, always and forever the only one who knows it, only I still don't understand anymore than I did then, what could be happening. I didn't understand what it could be.

With all those people around me or maybe it was just her, her and her bottle, laughing and laughing that awful laugh as she grabbed me or he grabbed me or maybe they grabbed me and they pushed me forward, pushed my head right into that part of her that was so big and so close while they made me take it in my mouth, she made me take it in my mouth that huge wrinkled part of her even if I didn't want to I kept my mouth closed and I tried not to breathe not to open my mouth but I couldn't keep doing it because I couldn't hold my breath any longer and I couldn't breathe through my nose my nose was pushed into her body so I did what I was told and I took it in my mouth and then when I did they pushed my head further in so my face was all wet and I was so scared that I went away then.

No matter how much fun I say it could be, no matter how much fun I would tell myself it was going to be no matter how much fun I might dream it could be touching myself in that one part of my body when I was all alone and waiting for when I would hear her calling Honey, Honey, come down here Honey, no matter how much I learned to call myself Honey, the way she did the way he did, the way they did, Honey Honey, sweet as Honey, dirty little Honey, and walk down the stairs ever so slowly while I fixed my smile on my face and told myself how good it was going to feel how nice it was going to be, no matter how I learned to hold onto that moment when someone would reach out and comfort me no matter how hard she laughed at me and called me names, no matter how much I did that, still. Still. I lost my name then. I lost it. My own name. I lost my name. The one I'd always felt so warm inside me. The one that made me feel special. When my mother hugged me.

I lost it.

And he was born.

That one who says he came from his father's head and he never had a mother, no mother at all, no mother at all, never any mother at all. To hug him or to love him. That there is just Lizzie who never was anyone's mother. Who he isn't like at all because he's never had anything at all between his legs, any more than Athena does, he's sure of that, much less any of those feelings down there, the ones that she had or that I would get, that I would feel even as I got sick and scared as she called my name as they called my name, Honey, come down here Honey, the feelings that will always be there, in that place no matter how far away I get. From Lizzie or from that room. But that arise whenever anyone calls me Honey or looks at me like that. With those eyes they had. And that breath. The feelings that he says he never has at all, never at all, because all he has is anger and hatred and more anger and more hatred and the desire to dismember us all. But mostly to dismember her, to tear her limb from limb to skin her like a rabbit, that one who gave birth to him no matter what he says. Because that's when he was born, from that moment that I moved my head away, all wet and sickly nauseous, he was born, a second me, full-blown from her body, from that one place, that one act, from that one kiss of terrible betrayal.

To keep inside himself all my fear and my pain, and to make it into anger and into hatred in some place far away from my body far away from our body, where all those feelings would arise while I would smile and beg and talk, and take into my mouth anything that I was asked, and let anything at all be done to that body as I told myself how much fun it was how very much fun it would always be in the end, while he would imagine inside himself inside that place far away and without a body, how he would dismember us all, all of us, all of us. Himself included.

Only he doesn't know why. He doesn't. Not really. No matter what he says I'm still the only one who does. Which is why I laugh at him and shout, I know something you don't know, I know something you don't know, I know something you don't know. Even if, no matter how much I search, I still can't find my name.

So that he chases me and I chase my name and I threaten to tell him and he threatens to kill me, and the space we inhabit together is full of dismembered bodies and the lives we live apart are full of terror, where he works and speaks and speaks and works and denies he has a body at all. While I, silenced by that same kiss that birthed him, say nothing, nothing at all. Even if I smile sometimes, or moan, or even whimper. Still I never speak. Except to him. To tease him, and to make him chase me, and to threaten to tell him, chanting I know something you don't know.

While all the time I wish I didn't. Know anything of this at all. Or that he could really do it. Choke us both. Into non-existence. Or back into the person we once were before that night. When there were no secrets to know. And no feelings to hide.

Because I would never have believed that it could turn out like this. I thought, just the way he did, that if we just got through it, we would be all right. Just the way I always knew it would be different in the morning and Lizzie would be my mother again and want to drink lots of milk and be kind, I thought that there would be one morning when it would be different forever. And there would be no Lizzie and no men and we could do whatever we wanted.

And maybe we can. Only we don't seem to want very much. What with him all sullen and angry, no matter how much he accomplishes, while those same feelings arise and arise between my legs the way they always did. The feelings that still make me want to lift up my skirt and show myself to the world, not just to him the way I do in our dreams. As I look down there, to contemplate that place where I look so much like Lizzie, that place where he was kissed into existence. Where those feelings start. The ones I feel now. All the time.

Even when I hug my children.

A GIFT

It will not cease, this need to explain your mother, though need itself, perhaps, needs a better term. If need was once the pounding red why why why in the gut, this has slowly become a mellow, pink, curiosity. Something you go back to every once in a while, the way you wear the last of those gifts she sent you. New this time. A sweatshirt, with a giant red fish. As you think of how the colours came back. Another day in the East Kootenays.

How you stood on a bridge, once more in September, and watched the Kokanee, the landlocked freshwater salmon, their heads bright red for the spawning season, move, not inexorably, nothing in that is any more predetermined than your survival, or anyone else's, who will make it and who not, even to spawn: Luck and contingency and — always — being in the right place at the right time.

Your mind will not even wander to that. To ask what the luck was that brought you there, safe, looking down. What you will see is how bright it is. How very bright the day, and that red, how it flashes and fragments against blue against black against green in the water. And you will laugh, knowing the colours are back only because Jane is with you. Jane Dark out of the dark, into the colours of the day now. Bringing them back to you. Herself the colours of the day now. Though still you will enjoy the conceit of your cupola room.

And as for your mother. That same day you will enter a pub, examine the ebullient local landscapes on the wall, the dart boards, the hockey game — or is it football, probably football — on TV, the guys laughing. And then, the one woman at the bar. Eccentric, dressed in old skirts and silver chains and bright makeup — the way Mickey does now — with everyone saying hello, stopping to squeeze her shoulder, or make a joke, or just to wink walking by. A regular, obviously a regular, without doubt a bit of a joke herself, you find yourself thinking. Even as you remember being a joke the nights of your mother's laughter, and the men's. Laughing at you, so that your body starts to shrink into itself, your shoulders hunching. Only the terror will not be there. It will not surface.

You will think only of how any older woman in a bar will always remind you of Mickey, even if you, now, are an older woman in a bar, drinking the dark ale you have learned you can drink without becoming her. And you will breathe deeply, and know, as the woman twirls and laughs and leaves — perhaps she is a local artist, perhaps the Sunday school teacher here for her Sunday pint after church, who knows — that you no longer have to make individuals you encounter take on symbolic meanings. Or even make the present day part of the past, worrying at why you should meet this ersatz Mickey now.

Your new knowledge will not stop you from indulging in one last fantasy. One last overarching fantasy. Perhaps better, a story frame. Incest and sexual abuse have become such typical — and topical — plot devices, you've gotten used to reading those stories of dissociation. Where some child, some adult feeling that child in her, in him, is always going off to the ceiling or the sky or the grass or just twenty feet into the air suspended as if by some small cord to her body, to which awful things continue to happen. A formula, which you always wonder if the writer is familiar with, or even perhaps, envies. And certainly real enough. Far too real, in fact. You know your own adventures along ceiling mouldings or tucked into the grouted edges of floor tiles. But easy too, just to write, the way you can just write anything, from nuclear holocaust to galaxy elimination to torture murder — instructions to move the plot along are as easy as instructions to get to the bank. So that such scenes can become merely a way to get things started, maybe a simple way to create a reason for the torture murder to come, or for that matter the galaxy elimination.

You think, too, as you read those stories, how you hear people repeat, We have only recently begun to acknowledge sexual abuse, while you think, Wasn't it always there? Talked — written — about. Certainly in literature. In biographies of celebrities. In the stories your friends told you. And also, already, as a plot device. The incest plot device, the sexual abuse plot device, have been around a long time. So, perhaps those stories, those books, were just put in such a way that no one but you took it seriously. All those priest jokes, those incest jokes, those Mommy Dearest jokes, like Lolita jokes, just that, jokes — anomalies, exceptions, no more. With nothing to say about us, all of us, nothing at all. No matter how frequent the occurrence. The way some of these books now, following a formula, make people want to stop taking it seriously again.

Oh, that, Isn't that old hat, they say, perhaps right after saying we've just begun to deal with it. While the Fight, the Makeover, the formula stories with just that soupçon of difficulty to make them interesting — but comforting — abound. Occupy both centre and periphery.

While sometimes you wonder if there's anyone out there so lucky as not to have had to do it, really, at least a little bit, that dissociation. Of course that's what people do, you remember saying the first time — and it's a long time ago now — you read of those things. Of course, everyone does that, you said, It's only natural. The way it was so familiar to know to do it, when first you had to when you confronted this material again. Your consciousness so easily tucked away in some far or hidden place.

You start to collect them. In detective fiction, speculative fiction, literary fiction. Cataloguing the different places the mind goes when abused. Some amusing, some horrific, some just bouncing the plot along. In a moment of sanity-saving perverse humour, you find yourself expanding on it. Wondering if a novel, some sort of fiction, could be built around this conceit: That there is a place abused children go to when they dissociate. Some form of common ground. Especially when it's heaven those children go to, or some other otherworldly place. Not just the corner of a room, or the space between the threads of someone's jacket, the burned spot in an old lampshade, but somewhere farther away. Another version of the grey cupola perhaps, though you would wish it prettier, nicer, bigger. But somehow angelic, so that you imagine it also pale pastels. So much an old English children's story, *The Secret Garden*, perhaps, or *Peter Rabbit*, that you wonder how many of those books were produced out of places of dissociation, out of escaping abuse.

A yellow room then, or better a field, suffused with pale yellow light like a morning mist, or a rose garden of dark pinks and rich greens so that light or dark the grey shimmering can still be there. In which she, your Jane, can be an old-fashioned doll of a girl, in the white lace she always longed for and could never admit to, with a large floppy white and yellow lace hat.

The children would only go there when the abuse arrived at its worst, only at its worst. You see it as a place filled with children in their best clothes, or the clothes they best dreamed of, but antique like her somehow, a vision out of Victoriana, boys in curls and shorts and those flat straw hats, girls in lace and a hat like hers or like those hats your aunt would get you for the Easter parade, straw with pastel cloth flowers to signal the coming of spring and your birthday, the end of winter and that awful period that was Mickey preparing her taxes.

Perhaps you could even broaden such a fantasy out to include traumatized children of all times and places, victims of whatever trauma, dressed to the nines of their own cultural imagination. In brilliant cotton huipiles or silk saris, wide silk pants or delicate wool sweaters, dashikis and djellabas, leather embroidered with delicately dyed porcupine quills, all prepared to play and to speak and to tell the best stories they know, in some universal language of the traumatized that everyone would be able to hear inside their heads. It would make another episodic novel. A book of examples. Moving from torture to witnessing the death of a village to being raped in a basement, foreign objects stuck up your anus.

The only problem, no matter what the garden, and you will remember thinking this, too, the first time you came up with this fantasy, is that in that universal shelter for abused children, it would be just as likely that you would meet Mickey there. And, for that matter, a whole bunch of those men. The way it would be just as likely for any child to meet her abuser there. Or his. Because you are sure there would be many boys — your brother, and AJ, too. But, of course, that's what would make it a story. Not just a heaven. The horror of that encounter generating narrative, generating story.

A story you certainly didn't want. So that you left your fantasy quickly. You were not the least prepared for the awful child Mickey. Even if that place might constrain her to honesty. Or memory. Yet you do keep coming back. Think, maybe you will make it into your version of that Cortázar story you have spoken of so often, the one that angered Jane so that it made her speak. With its meeting beyond death of victimizer and victim, in some pure place before damage, when they could reach out for each other with unconditional love. A story whose only justification, you once told a friend, was that they were dead. You liked that. The sense that when time ceases, all understanding is possible. Probably because consequences have become examples, thoughts, concepts, not pain.

You do like the idea that there is such a place beyond — or perhaps it's within — dissociation, a place where all the wounds, including those that perpetuate the cycle of abuse, would, temporarily, just for that dissociated instant, be healed. Giving, perhaps, some small energy with which to carry on, to some part of the self, but nothing so large as to ever be an epiphany, an enlightenment. Just enough innocent playful energy would be infused through that field's toys and balloons and cuddly animals and warm yellow love to allow the child to go on. To survive. Upon his or her return into chronological time from that particular place in story.

You will laugh at yourself, of course. You know full well that contingent as we are in this world, story world or no story world, there is no such place of healing, however briefly. And no such undead human love so wide as to allow for this. Not into the here and now will there enter this imagined place beyond. Not for more than an instant. Perhaps only long enough to see the yellow light but never the toys.

You are not convinced it should enter. Not with this world's need for well-directed anger and for change. For telling the good guys from the bad. No matter how many the shades of grey. Cold discerning eyes are sometimes needed to make out what it is that lies beneath the Trickster's change of form. If it was up to you, at least a part of you, you would wind up wishing to blow such a world up, just so that those who would wind up perpetuating the worst abuses would receive no input of energy to help them survive to do so.

You will realize that this fantasy is just another version of what you have always wanted or needed, in your attempts to save Mickey in order to save yourself: That unconditional parental love that assures us the world is a safe place. So what better, more poignant way to say this, than to make a story of such a place, a heavenly shelter where abused children could care for each other? In that place to which they would all, in their worst moments, flee.

And what better idea could there be than that of a universal comfort, a place of rest, for everyone.

This fantasy will not be what changes things. Rather, it will be a by-product of your new ease with yourself. It seems so easy now to survive without her. That's why you call the hospital when she contracts pneumonia. It is just such an easy thing to do. Nothing twists in you as you do it. Though you will not envy your brother his role as caregiver when the diazepams prescribed upon her release turn her back into the Mickey monster again. Though it is only later in her last illness that he will tell you that there is a tone of voice — that gurgling in her throat — that forces him to abandon the room, his mind, if not his hands, shaking.

While you will see her again briefly that one time you go to New York for a school reunion, and you will talk her through the morning of September 11th, 2001, the two of you hearing the roar of Tower Two coming down as it rattles the windows of that house it was so hard for you to leave. A friend who had witnessed the first plane into the towers from her barge had called Mickey, and she had called you.

Exactly four months later, she will be dead. You ask yourself what effect the sifting debris had on her compromised lungs.

This new reality on her aging mind.

After her death you will return to stay in the house for the first time in over twenty years. And, too, you will enter the basement. And you will walk down the stairs you could not walk down, even in your mind, the ones that made you leave that exercise so quickly during therapy. That place redolent of horror. And of voices.

And they will all be there. Voices. So many voices. Sealed inside those old filing cabinets. All the papers she has kept all these years, that she had kept asking you to sort, to take care of.

You have promised yourself that you will not sort them. You will exercise your duty of care merely by taking them out of the old cabinets where they are slowly crumbling and mildewing, to move them into plastic boxes. From there they can be taken out and archived. Maybe through the *New Yorker* where Mark worked, or the waterfront societies on whose boards Mickey spent her last years.

Still, you won't be able to stop yourself. Your hands will start to open books, pour contents out of envelopes, your eyes to read.

You will be able to talk about it later as a found book. Some literary part of you terribly taken with it. The way you are with your fantasy. This idea of the history between the lines. Something very like the fragmented novels of Manuel Puig. A voice, voices, from the forties, from the fifties, a kind of voice, Hepburnesque in its diction, that will never be heard again. Perky, resolute, and in consummate denial. And all of this in four scrapbooks, taking in all the years of her marriage and prior to her marriage: her first years in New York, first as Mickey Green, and then Mickey Murphy, girl reporter.

Acceptance letters, rejection letters, letters from sources from bosses from rivals from friends. Her interviews, her reviews, her articles. Mark's articles, his reviews, the reviews of his books. Reviews of their Brooklyn anthology, complete with photo, the two of them sitting, faces together, the book held out. Mickey in a tiny hat with a veil. Then, in between it all, other voices enter. Letters offering to adopt you, notes telling Mark to clear out, letters fighting for custody, reports on drunken evenings, on the police coming — your dad there too, if on the margins, as he will ever be in her narrative of herself, but there, his twenty-forth birthday in the house.

At the end of the last book appears Mark's death in South Africa. The letters looking for him, the telegrams to tell that he was found, his last greetings to you and to Tim, the notices of his funeral to which you were not taken, and then as the books end, the fight for the return of Mark's Veterans' benefits, the evidence of the battle between Mickey and Mark's sister over you and your brother. Then there is no more careful pasting of articles onto the page, even of the contradictory letters and notes placed carefully between. Now, as she loses control — control and her job to the spiral of ever worsening drinking — papers are stuffed helter-skelter into nine-by-twelve manila envelopes. The way they will be for fifty years.

And there, in the first envelope that ends nineteen-fifty-two, the year of Mark's death, there are the three letters to her psychiatrist, the one she left, she said, because she could not afford him, just, she always said, as she was reaching a break-through. You and Tim were more important, she said, she just had to quit. While you have always thought it was precisely because she was reaching a breakthrough that she had to quit. Now, you think, looking at the evidence, it was because the custody battle had been won. She had proven herself a fit mother. Or one who was trying very hard.

Mostly the letters speak of her affair with Paul Garcia, the working-class Mexican lover, the one who lived in the basement you now stand in, who invited you down, to play at games you did not understand among his sheets. Her psychiatrist has somehow classified him as the depth of her rebellion, as if to love someone of a lower social class than yours were always somehow tawdry. She replies that no, no, he was hardly the worst, certainly not so very self-destructive, she was capable of a great deal more evil than that, the worst was how in acute anxiety she would find the most down-and-out, the most brutal or brutalized of men, and bring them home. Just as you have said.

And then. At the very end. She tries to explain it: She names her own abuser.

The next morning you will wake up sick. There on what for thirty years has been your mother's bed. What, before that was the cloak room, the breakfast nook. Her whole apartment just that: The kitchen and the cloak room. Ever since she renovated the house and rented the rest to the new yuppies of the district, so different from the roomers of the fifties. You think, for a moment, that you have fallen asleep on the old wooden bench of the booth. Sit up, wondering why.

Then, when you've remembered where you are, why you're there, you think about how bad you feel and decide it must be the mildew, the dust, the heat, the lack of air circulation.

When you remember the basement you will be furious. As you often were, as you would feel tricked by what seemed an affectionate invitation turned to abuse. What in the world had she meant? What had she been attempting to do to you? All that time insisting you must come do the archives. What if you really had? What if you'd come into this unprepared? An innocent retracing her steps like that day in therapy. What if you hadn't known there could be anything down there? What if you hadn't done the intense work of the last years?

You think you would have been immobilized. Caught here.

The way your brother will soon be immobilized by the house. His unsorted memories, you think, pinning him there. And his need, too, to protect her the way he always did. You think she might have intended for you to stay there. To build a monument to her. With those archives. Caught once more, in making her life the centre of yours. Dedicating yourself, the way you did for years, to figuring her out. The way you still do sometimes. Going back to that why, why, why.

Later, you will speak to your brother. Trying to make those archives into a kind of joking comment on her character, the way over the years, so much communication in the house has been encoded in Mickey jokes. You will both ask yourselves, what it was that made her preserve these things, but never say, never confirm any of it. Always say she did not remember, or dismiss all claims out of hand.

You will smile at each other. The kind of conspiracy of your best days. Before he, enduring the same abuse, changed the rules. When you would hide together as she danced and made fun of you, try to pour her liquor down the sink in the butler's pantry after it was delivered, by the man from the liquor store who in solidarity with his helplessness helped Tim build model airplanes. And you will continue to talk like on the best of those nights, for many many hours. And you will create the same mood you did then. Make it an adventure. Telling Mickey stories, not to understand, but like going to war. Bragging at what you have survived.

Waking up late the next day, you will remember exactly where you are. You will dress and get ready to leave quickly, the way you did on so many mornings after. Moving further and further away, staying away longer and longer as you got older. Until by the time you left for university it was weeks.

Today, it is only out to the Promenade. Six blocks to the exclusive view of lower Manhattan unique to the Heights, that always posh neighbourhood your mother's block has now been gentrified into. You breathe deeply, the way you always did there. Or sitting out on the girders of the Brooklyn Bridge, planning your escape.

You think how easy it is to breathe. Despite the memories. Despite the basement. How you turned to your brother, the night before, a night before only of memories, memories within your control, and said: That's all I ever asked her to acknowledge. And how you smiled a wan and twisted smile.

In the noon sunshine it will occur to you that she has. She has acknowledged your claim. Staring out at the buildings of Lower Manhattan, the skyline now so like the skyline you would see from there as a child, you will note that even if little appears to have changed, so much has. Despite your earlier reaction, the colours are still there, and Jane with you as you walk. In fact, it has been years now since you have entered that place of grey, of pain so profound you were unsure as to how to make it through the day or the night or even the next few minutes. So long in fact, that you can barely believe yourself that you have ever felt that way, that such pain is possible, feel your statements of it hard to edit, hard to believe. Even if you now know that it was true, the pain, and all your memories. Or perhaps the pain has ceased because you know. And it no longer matters in any significant way whether she acknowledged you or not.

Yesterday's purple red blow to the gut was only a brief reminder. You feel no temptation to remove the compromising letters, the compromising notes, from the scrapbooks or the envelopes. No temptation to rebuild that other narrative with its chipper reviews and clever asides. You feel safe in your knowledge. Safe where you are. Even looking at that devastated skyline, the terror alert once more to red, the army helicopters circling, you feel safe, safe. And it does not even seem a miracle, but just a fact. She can no longer reach you, tear apart your narrative. Take you, the teller, from the centre of your tale.

You will return to your fantasy then. Imagine her, some part of her, in that secret pastel garden, and you will imagine her — that girl that Mickey once was — reaching from there into real time to make sure that this would never be destroyed. And you will think, perhaps, that that was the best of her, and think again of those two reviews. And you will not know what part of her it is that has done this, but suddenly you will look upon it not as another burden but as a gift. That while it is true that she could never say this, still she would not destroy it, leaving instead the document to testify to how denial and destruction and self-hatred work, even if she could not tell it herself, could not even speak to it. And that leaving those documents there, was itself a form of truth telling.

You will recognize inside this inability to destroy any document, the loyalty to narrative truth that has allowed you to get through — to pull yourself from chaos. And for a moment, you will thank her for that gift, even if what you had to survive was so often caused by her.

You will feel it again then too, how it will echo there, that name first encountered in her letter to her psychiatrist, that you will see again and again in her early diaries, even at her mother's funeral, the name of that one man who abused her, who, she thought, generated the cycle of self abuse. That piece of a terrible history that she has passed beyond herself to you, marked it on your body. So that you wonder too, what his story was, moving back in time, to the generation before and before and before, through a culture saturated not with sex but hatred of sex: Saturated with sexual abuse. You see her abuser's name, over and over. A perfect name, one that would be laughed at in a fictional tale: Mr. Butcher. You think of its effect, feel it echo. A history in a word.

    Butcher.

    Butcher.

    Butcher.

    Butcher.

    Butcher.

You look out at the river. At the buildings beyond. You speak it out loud. Loose it to the wind.

    Butcher.

Translator, interpreter, teacher, community activist, award winning visual artist and acclaimed author of six books, Sarah Murphy is the recipient of the 2003 Howard O'Hagan Award for her book of performance monologues, drawings and photomontage, *die tinkerbell die,* published during an international residency with the Word Hoard in West Yorkshire in 2002. The present collection is part of a cycle of work that has included her self-illustrated novel, *Connie Many Stories*, a finalist for the Georges Bugnet Award, and the *scrapbook* installation, presented in both Canada and England. Previous work has also included *Lilac in Leather* (Pedlar, 1998), a novel of love and betrayal in the New York art world of the 1970s, also a finalist for the George Bugnet Award; and *The Measure of Miranda*, a story of the Latin American terror regimes of the 1980s, and the Canadians who, like Murphy, worked in solidarity with their victims. Presently, she is working on a novel of the Mexican student movement of 1968, in which she participated, as well as on a further series of performance monologues.

ACKNOWLEDGEMENTS

The Forgotten Voices of Jane Dark is one of those books long in the making — in the thinking, the writing, the assembling, the waiting, the changing — of book and story and world. As such it has encountered much assistance, much support — as well as much difficulty — along its way, a twisting road full of switchbacks and tangled undergrowth as well as occasional clear vision. From its inception as small stories designed not for publication but only to allow me to see myself, to its final editing, many have helped me develop not just the writing but the insight into the issues dealt with, as well as into myself. I would like to thank all of them. From the anonymous members of support groups in which I took part, to the publishers and conference organizers who first took the work seriously as literature, to the members of the Alberta College of Art and Design and the Centre Gallery who believed in the possibility of a visual narrative, to the unknown readers of the published stories who have wished me well, many have been with me in this process. In particular I would like to thank my close friends, Leila Sujir and Marie Jakober, who first looked at the first stories; Guadalupe Otero who acknowledged the work from Mexico; Pat Clarke, my therapist, who was with me throughout; Barb Bickel and Cathy Cruz, the artists who saw where art and healing are one; Bill Sherar, my dad, who ameliorated the worst times in both childhood and its memory, and gave me much needed information; Mark, Lucero and Lee, my children, who afforded me such insight and showed me such patience; Margot Adler, my oldest childhood friend, who could recognize me here; the Yorkshire crew, Keith Jafrate and Dianne Darby and Bob Lockwood and the others who gave me new insight into my work as well as unique opportunities to do it; Roberta Rees and Claire Harris and Edna Alford and Caterina Edwards and Lynette D'Anna and all the other writers who helped with the work along the way; Bev Daurio who hived off *Connie Many Stories* to make it a novel; Beth Follett who finally took up putting this all together — stories and essays from first nightmare to last trip to New York, cellar to cellar so to speak; and all the forgotten voices inside me and out who have been with me, too. And most especially to Tom Proudlock, my partner of twenty-eight years, who was with me from the nights I hid in our closets, to the first moments I sent out my manuscripts, to when, once more, I was able to laugh and walk freely. Tom, who, in spirit, is with me still — This is the one you should have been here for.